THE
DRAGON
DETECTIVE
AGENCY

THE CASE OF THE
VANISHED SEA DRAGON

THE CASE OF THE VANISHED SEA DRAGON

GARETH P. JONES

BLOOMSBURY

First published in Great Britain in 2008 by Bloomsbury Publishing Plc,
36 Soho Square, London, W1D 3QY

A CIP catalogue record of this book is available from the British Library
ISBN 978 0 7475 9555 7

Printed and bound in Great Britain by Clays Ltd, St Ives Plc

1 3 5 7 9 10 8 6 4 2

All papers used by Bloomsbury Publishing are natural, recyclable products made from
wood grown in well-managed forests. The manufacturing processes conform
to the environmental regulations of the country of origin.

Chapter One

The double-chinned security guard sat slumped in front of a wall of black and white TV screens. He opened his bleary eyes, yawned and pulled a doughnut from the box, biting into it and licking a globule of jam that dribbled down his chin. He was unaware that every move he made was being watched by a four-metre-long (from nose to tail), red-backed, green-bellied, urban-based Mountain Dragon, who was perfectly camouflaged against the sloping rooftop across the road.

Dirk Dilly, the dragon detective, gazed longingly at the doughnuts. He was starving. To take his mind off his rumbling stomach he opened his book at a chapter called 'Dragon Births' and read.

Once impregnated, the female dragon travels deep into the earth's belly to the banks of the Outer Core, where she lays the egg. She then picks it up in her mouth and dives into the liquid fire. This is an extremely painful experience. The mother plants the egg deep in the liquid fire and returns to the shores, where she waits for her youngling to hatch and swim to the surface.

Dirk examined an illustration of pregnant dragons waiting for their newborns to appear from the bubbling underground lake.

A Sea Dragon mother places her egg relatively near the surface of the fiery lake, giving its offspring's skin the ability to soften in water. A Mountain Dragon's egg is planted deeper into the lava, making the child's back tougher and its flame stronger. Of all subspecies it is the Sky Dragon that buries its egg deepest.

It takes weeks for a young Skyling to swim to the surface, by which time the fire has become an integral part of its composition, giving it the rare power known as 'sublimation'. This is the ability to instantaneously turn its entire body into cloud-like gas.

Dirk looked up from the book. Nothing had changed. The screens still showed the interior of an art gallery located above a doughnut shop in a busy London street. Being night-time the doors were locked, but they may well have stayed locked during the days for all the visitors the art gallery got. In spite of its central location few passers-by knew of its existence and even fewer bothered to go up. Most were more interested in the selection of mouth-watering, calorie-laden sugar-coated dough-nuts downstairs than the drab paintings upstairs.

Dirk had been watching the gallery every night since he got the call from a plummy-voiced man who had introduced himself as Mr Strettingdon-Smythe, the curator of the galley.

'Important pieces are going missing,' Mr Strettingdon-Smythe said over the phone.

'Don't you have security?' replied Dirk, holding the receiver between his shoulder and his long pointy ear and reaching for his glass of neat orange squash.

'Yes, but he's useless, always asleep on the job.'

'Why don't you fire him?' asked Dirk, draining the contents of the glass.

'I wish I could but he's a relative of the owner.'

'What about CCTV?'

'Every room is monitored but the picture goes fuzzy whenever a painting goes missing, like it's being . . .' Mr Strettingdon-Smythe paused, reaching for the right word, '. . . interfered with somehow.'

'Why don't you go to the police?' asked Dirk.

'The owner says it's bad for business. I can't see how business could be any worse. Hardly anyone ever comes to the gallery. Perhaps we should show pictures of doughnuts,' said the curator bitterly.

Mr Strettingdon-Smythe explained that there had been four thefts so far, each following the same pattern. Late at night the CCTV would go haywire for around an hour, while the thieves removed one painting without breaking a window, setting off the alarmed door or showing any signs of forced entry. In each case the broken frame was left behind. Only the picture itself was taken.

It sounded intriguing. Dirk agreed to take on the case.

'And, Mr Dilly,' added Mr Strettingdon-Smythe, 'I'd appreciate utmost discretion. I haven't told the owner I hired you. I know he would disapprove but I can't bear to have any more pieces go missing. Please don't let anyone see you.'

'Believe me, it would be a bigger problem for me

than for you if I got seen,' replied Dirk, hanging up.

His first thought was that it had to be an inside job. The obvious suspect was the double-chinned security guard but, after a few days following him, Dirk uncovered no signs of guilt. During the day he worked on the security desk of an office building. He had a cheery nature and enjoyed greeting every employee by name. After a full day's work he headed to the art gallery, via the doughnut shop, and spent the evening stuffing his face and dozing off. He was incompetent but he wasn't corrupt.

The question that bothered Dirk was why the thieves didn't take the whole lot in one go? Why take one painting at a time, risking capture with each return visit? It didn't make any sense and, after almost two weeks staking out the gallery, Dirk was no closer to getting any answers.

He opened his book and read another paragraph.

The only way to tell if a Sky Dragon has recently materialised is by the dragon-shaped trace of ash it leaves behind on the ground. However, the process of changing from solid matter into a gas state and vice versa is painful and not one Sky Dragons do lightly. Precious little is known about Sky Dragons (even amongst other dragons), although some claim that they can distil water from the clouds and create powerful walls of fire out of nowhere.

Since dragonkind went into hiding it is generally believed that all of the world's Sky Dragons have remained in a 'sublimated' state.

So whenever you notice a dragon-shaped cloud drifting across the sky you are probably looking at a Sky Dragon.

The book was called *Dragonlore* and it was written by his landlady's late husband, Ivor Klingerflim. It worried Dirk that a human could know so much about dragons. There was a chapter on eating habits, correctly identifying all dragons as vegetarians. There were chapters on how different types of dragon varied in appearance, strength and powers. It was correct in every detail, such as the ability to blend being a skill unique to Mountain Dragons, or yellow-backed Scavengers having extremely bad breath, due to their diet of cow manure and garlic. There were even types of dragon he had never encountered, like the Californian Desert Dragons, who apparently had spikes sticking out of their backs and spat poison instead of breathing fire.

He had no idea how Ivor had learnt so much, but was relieved when Mrs Klingerflim had said that he could only afford to print a hundred or so copies.

'He spent his whole life studying dragons,' she explained.

'So weren't you surprised when you discovered that I was one?' Dirk asked, feeling foolish, always having assumed that Mrs Klingerflim's poor eyesight was the reason that she didn't scream when she first saw him.

'Very little surprises you when you get to my age,' replied the old lady, 'except for ice cream.'

'Ice cream?' said Dirk.

'Oh yes, all the new flavours they keep bringing out. Cheesecake this and monkey nuts that. I can't keep up. We only had vanilla, chocolate and strawberry when I was a little girl. Ivor used to say that one day he would invent a beer-flavoured ice cream and make his millions. He was a silly man,' she said fondly. 'Mind you,' she added with a wink, 'I wouldn't be surprised if there is such a thing now.'

The double-chinned security guard fell asleep, dropping the half-eaten doughnut on to the floor. Dirk was about to open the book again when he noticed the CCTV screens flicker and the picture disappear.

13

He checked the street below. At the bus stop a few late-night party-goers were waiting for the night bus home, eating revolting-looking kebabs, and dripping chilli sauce on the pavement. None of them looked up. Londoners rarely did.

He flew to the large window and peered inside the gallery. There was no sign of a break-in but, on the far wall, a painting of a sad-looking lady had fallen to the floor, shattering the glass.

Dirk pushed his nose to the window and saw the picture lift itself out of the frame and move across the floor.

He pushed the window open and entered the gallery. It was risky but he knew the CCTV cameras were still out. Standing on his hind legs, he surveyed the gallery. No sign of anyone. In one corner of the room was a small red light. He bent down and inspected it. The light was coming from a black sphere about the size of a golf ball. Dirk picked it up.

'So that's how they're scrambling the cameras,' he said to himself.

He tucked the black sphere behind his wing and noticed a second blinking light on a white box attached to the ceiling. Realising what it was, he clasped his paw over his nostrils but it was too late to stop the thin line of grey smoke drift up from his nose, through the room, into a vent in the small box. Dirk knew exactly what would happen now. The smoke particles would neutralise the ions, causing a drop in current between the two plates in the ionisation chamber, triggering the smoke alarm.

'Rats,' he muttered, as the ringing sound filled the room. Case or no case, he couldn't afford to be seen by a human. He got to the window and jumped to the roof across the road. The double-chinned security guard entered the room, holding a bucket of sand, with dried jam smeared across both chins. Not noticing the painting moving across the floor, the large man tripped over it, sending the bucket in the air, spraying sand across the room, before landing with a CLUNK on the floor.

Dirk blended with the roof, where he could see that the security cameras had come back on and were recording the farcical scene inside the gallery from various angles. Dirk was relieved he had got out in time. To be seen by a human was to breach the forbidden divide between dragonkind and mankind. Mrs Klingerflim and Holly were human, of course, but that was different. Mrs K and Holly were his friends.

Chapter Two

Holly Bigsby got off the bus at the stop near her house and hastily headed down the road in the opposite direction.

'Oi, Holly Hockey Sticks,' shouted Archie Snellgrove, following her off the bus.

She quickened her pace.

'Are we going for tea and scones?' jeered Archie's ginger-haired friend, in what Holly guessed was supposed to be a posh voice.

She didn't turn her head. She had to lose them. If Archie discovered where she lived he would make the whole summer a nightmare. He had certainly gone out of his way to make her last two months as miserable as possible.

When she had arrived at Gristle Street Comprehensive, Archie had honed in on her like a heat-seeking missile, taking every available opportunity to humiliate her in public and make his friends laugh. He started off with fairly general jokes but when he had learnt that her dad had worked for the Ministry of Defence he quickly worked it into his routine.

'Hey, Bigsby, will you lend us a hand . . .' he would start before pausing for comic effect, pushing his dirty blond hair away from his face then adding, '. . . grenade? A hand grenade, get it? . . . Oi, Biggles, is it true you've got bullet-proof pants? . . . Oi, Beggars-be, do you keep your fish in a fish tank or an armoured tank?'

Holly was determined not to rise to it. She couldn't afford to get into trouble. Dad had made it clear that even though he had lost his job and they didn't have as much money coming in now, one step out of line and she would be packed off back to William Scrivener School, which she had hated because it was so far away from her home and her cat, Willow, and her only friend, Dirk Dilly.

More recently Archie had grown tired of army jokes

and decided she must be posh, taunting her with names like 'Posh Girl', 'Lady Penelope' and his new favourite, 'Holly Hockey Sticks'.

She didn't know what grudge he had against her but she was sure she hadn't done anything to deserve it. Every single evening he followed her home, trying to discover where she lived, so he could extend her torment beyond school hours, but every time she had managed to lose him.

Finally, the end of term had come. There would be no more Archie for six weeks, providing she could lose him one more time. She glanced at the boys in a car wing mirror, making sure she had enough time for a getaway.

'Will mummy be making caviar for tea?' shouted Archie, making his friend laugh.

This upset Holly more than Archie could have known. She drew a deep breath. Letting Archie know that her mum was dead would give him months' worth of material.

Besides, Holly didn't talk to anyone about her mum's death. Not even her dad. Holly sped up. She needed just a little more distance to lose Archie and his friend.

'Is one in a hurry? Does one need to feed the

corgis?' shouted Archie, laughing loudly.

Holly broke into a run, turning a corner and another into a drive that led to a row of garages. She ran full pelt towards them. It was a dead end.

Archie's friend yelled, 'She's gone down there.'

Their approaching footsteps echoed around the walls. She ran to the garage door in the far corner and pushed herself against it. They were almost within sight. With all her concentration she focused on what it would feel like to be a dark green garage door.

Archie and his friends rounded the corner and stopped in their tracks.

'Where did she go?' exclaimed Archie.

'She must have gone over the roofs,' said his friend.

'How could she have done? No one's that quick. We'd be able to see her climbing up there.'

'What else could she have done?'

'I dunno.' Archie grinned. 'Maybe she can fly.'

'That's mental,' said his friend.

Archie looked at the garages. His pale blue eyes drifted past Holly. He scratched his head in confusion, ruffling his dirty blond hair.

'Maybe she's invisible,' he suggested.

'People can't turn invisible,' scoffed his friend.

Holly wasn't invisible. Not entirely. If Archie and his

friend had looked carefully they would have seen her brown eyes and the faint outline of the girl, standing perfectly blended with the garage door behind her.

Archie said, 'She's quick. I'll give her that. She ain't here. Come on.'

Holly waited until they were gone then smiled, causing her mouth to reappear. Certain that no one was watching she shifted, and her natural colour returned completely. She had never intended to taste dragon blood. She had only been trying to identify the sticky green liquid that had rubbed off Dirk's injured body when he had come to find her at her last school. She certainly hadn't known that by tasting Dirk's blood she would gain some of his powers, but, over the last couple of months, she had become increasingly grateful for this extra advantage she had over Archie Snellgrove.

Chapter Three

Dirk felt annoyed with himself. He should have known about the fire alarm. He was on the familiar route back to his office, jumping from rooftop to rooftop, somersaulting to a school building and diving off the edge, spreading his wings, gliding down to a row of houses, running across them, over a busy road, checking the street below before soaring through the open window.

It was such a familiar route that he could have done it blindfolded, which was why it came as such a surprise when he crashed headfirst into something inside his office.

'Owmph,' he exclaimed as the rest of his body

caught up with his face.

Dirk had no idea what he had hit but it was soft and unstable and moving backwards. He grabbed what felt like a pair of shoulders, lifted his head and found himself face to face with a rather startled-looking Sea Dragon, staggering precariously backwards through his office.

Dirk wasn't exactly the tidiest of dragons. Old newspapers, case files, discarded orange-squash bottles and empty baked bean tins littered the floor. The Sea Dragon tripped, losing its footing, sending Dirk flying over its head, in a move that would have scored top marks in a judo competition.

The second object that Dirk collided with was considerably harder than the first. It was his filing cabinet. The cabinet rocked. The TV that rested on top, toppled and fell on his head.

'Oof,' he uttered, quickly grabbing it to prevent it smashing, then placing it carefully back.

He rubbed his head, stood up and found the light switch. He couldn't see the other dragon but there was only one place in his office big enough for a dragon to hide. Under his desk. He knew this because when, not so long ago, Holly had barged into his office uninvited it was where he had hidden. It was the largest desk he had been able to find in the mail-order catalogue but even so he had found it a squeeze to get under. His tail could be curled round to take minimum space. The neck was also squashable. It was his large belly that had proved difficult. For this reason, Dirk knew how the Sea Dragon was feeling. The pins and needles would have already started and soon the cramp would follow.

'Hello, Mister Dilly,' called Mrs Klingerflim on the landing. 'Is everything all right in there?'

'Fine, Mrs K,' responded Dirk. 'Just clumsy old me.'

'Right-oh. Call if you want anything. I'll be putting the kettle on in a minute.'

'OK,' said Dirk. 'Thanks, Mrs K.'

Dirk dropped on to all fours and approached the desk. He picked up a bottle of orange squash and poured himself a glass.

'Whoever you are you shouldn't be here,' he said. 'You know the punishment for breaching the forbidden divide.'

Around a thousand years ago at a conference held high in the Himalayas, the dragon world had voted on whether to hide from mankind or to destroy them before they became too strong. Those in favour of fighting rose into the air and became known as up-airers. Minertia, the greatest dragon of all, counted the votes and announced that all dragons would retreat to remote corners of the earth until mankind's time was past. Attacking a human, being seen by a human or allowing a human to find evidence of dragons were outlawed, punishable by banishment to the Inner Core.

Ironically, many centuries later, Minertia herself was convicted of breaking her own law and banished.

'You know, there's very little point hiding when you've already been seen,' said Dirk.

The Sea Dragon said nothing.

'OK, here's what I know about you,' said Dirk. 'You're a Sea Dragon; you recently left the sea in a hurry and travelled to London specifically to find me.'

The desk wobbled and the Sea Dragon's head appeared.

'How are you knowing this?' she said. It was a female, with some kind of accent. Dirk wasn't sure what, maybe Spanish.

'Well, it's not difficult to see you're a Sea Dragon. The gills are a dead giveaway. A Sea Dragon's back hardens with time out of water, but your back is still soft. Usually you would hide out until it hardens, but you didn't, so you were in a hurry. I can't believe that your presence under my desk is a coincidence, which means you came specifically looking for me.' Dirk blew a smoke ring. 'How did I do?'

'Everything you say is right, but I do not understand how you can live with the humano,' she said.

Until recently Dirk could have shrugged this off, saying that Mrs K had no idea he was anything other than an unreliable human tenant with a heavy smoking habit. He pulled out his copy of *Dragonlore* from behind his wing and placed it on the desk.

'What do you want?' he snapped.

The Sea Dragon climbed out from under the desk and cricked her back. 'I am wanting the help from you.'

'What sort of help?'

'Detective help,' she replied, 'like you give the humanos. My name is Alba Longs. My sister, Delfina, has gone vanished. I was supposed to be meeting with her in Spain but she is gone. I am needing you to help finding her.'

'I don't take cases from dragons,' replied Dirk. 'They're too much trouble and they don't pay well.'

'I have gold to pay you,' she said, reaching behind her wing and holding out several lumps of gold.

Dirk inspected them. 'Look, that's great in the

dragon world, but I can't exactly pay the rent in gold, can I?'

Alba looked confused. 'I do not know what is this the rent but you must help me. I have no one else to be asking.'

'Do I look like I give a rat's banjo? You shouldn't be this close to humans. It's not safe.'

'But you are living with them and speaking with them and making work with them.'

Dirk didn't like how much this Sea Dragon knew about him. 'I can blend and I'm experienced. If you get spotted, your lost sister will be the least of your problems. If you get seen we're talking full-scale war.'

'I do not want that but I must find my sister.'

Alba was prowling around the room, inspecting the strange objects she found on the floor. She picked up an unopened tin of chilli-flavoured baked beans. 'What is this?' she asked.

'My dinner,' replied Dirk tersely.

'Food? I am starving,' she said, biting into it, sending beans and chilli tomato sauce across the room, splattering the walls and catching Dirk in the eye. Alba chewed and swallowed the tin.

'I very like it,' she said, burping, 'but the shell is too crunchy.'

Dirk wiped the sauce away from his eyes.

'Ooh, what is this?' she asked, picking up the TV remote control.

'Leave my stuff alone,' barked Dirk. 'I've told you, I can't help you find –'

Dirk's words were drowned out by the TV, which Alba had managed to turn on. There was a music show on. A group of scruffy-looking teenagers were playing guitars and screaming, '*We're louder than a juggernaut / We're crazy like a fox / We're playing our guitars / And not wearing any socks.*'

Petrified by the noise, Alba threw the remote control behind her and ran at the TV. Dirk tried to block her but she whacked him in the ear and leapfrogged over him.

'Stop the loudnesses,' she screamed, knocking the TV off its resting spot. Dirk attempted to catch it but Alba was in his way and he watched helplessly as it fell to the ground. The fall smashed the screen but the speakers were unaffected and the rock band continued to sing.

'*We do whatever we want / Beg, steal or borrow / We were rocking all of yesterday / And we'll carry on tomorrow. Yeah.*'

'The loudnesses . . . Make the loudnesses stop,' yelled Alba.

A pounding came on the door.

'Mr Dilly, are you all right?' It was Mrs Klingerflim.

'Fine, Mrs K. Sorry, it's my TV,' he replied.

'Well, it's quite noisy, dear.'

'Yes, I'll turn it down,' replied Dirk.

'*Fish still swim, birds still fly, rock's still rock and I'm still I.*'

Another banging started, this one from the adjacent wall. A voice shouted, 'Keep the bleeding noise down or I'll call the bleeding police.'

BANG BANG.

'Make the loudnesses stop.'

BANG BANG BANG.

'*We don't care what our parents say / They're far too old and sad.*'

BANG BANG BANG BANG.

'The loudnesses.'

'*We just wanna rock all day / So leave it out, Mum and Dad.*'

BANG BANG BANG BANG BANG.

'Stop the loudnesses.'

'*Yeah, yeah, yeah, we wanna rock.*'

'Oi! You're disturbing the bleeding peace.'

'Mr Dilly, the neighbours are complaining.'

BANG BANG BANG BANG BANG BANG.

Dirk's head felt like it was going to cave in, and just when he thought it couldn't get any louder, the phone started to ring.

Chapter Four

Since losing his seat at the election the previous month Holly's dad had spent most of his days moping about in his pyjamas watching daytime television, so Holly was surprised to return home to find him standing in the hallway, cleanly shaven, wearing a suit, adjusting his tie in the mirror.

He glanced at her in the usual way, as though identifying who she was before getting back to more important matters, in this case, the straightness of his tie. It was the same way he looked at Willow.

'Hello, erm . . . Holly,' he said, undoing the tie and starting again.

'What's going on?' she asked.

Dad's big-haired wife stepped into the hallway from the kitchen, her hair looking even bigger than usual. 'We have a very important guest coming tonight. I need you on your best behaviour,' she said, holding a tray of very neatly arranged tiny morsels of food. A small furry white face with a black smudge on its nose followed her out of the kitchen.

'Keep your cat away from my canapés,' she said accusingly.

Seeing Holly, Willow purred and rubbed herself against her leg. Holly picked her up.

'What guest?' she asked.

'Only Brant Buchanan,' Big Hair replied proudly.

'Who's Brant Buchanan?' asked Holly.

'Who is Brant Buchanan?' squawked Big Hair incredulously. 'Only the seventh richest man in the world, that's who. They say he makes so much money that if he dropped a thousand pounds on the floor, by the time he picked it up he would have earned it back ten times over. He owns three islands.'

'I've never heard of him.'

'His company, Global Sands, employs more people worldwide than the entire population of Belgium.'

Holly shrugged. 'What do they do?'

Big Hair took the tray into the front room and

placed it on the coffee table. 'Look him up on the Internet if you're so interested. You'll have to keep yourself out of the way. Tonight could make a big difference. If all goes well your father could get a job out of it.'

'Doing what?' Holly asked her dad, who was still struggling with his tie.

'Never mind that,' said his wife. 'Your father is capable of many things if he puts his mind to it. What are you doing with that, Malcolm? Let me do it.' She slapped his hands away and tied his tie for him.

In her room, Holly changed out of her school uniform then switched on her computer, while Willow occupied herself chasing a fly around the room. She typed 'Global Sands' into the search engine and found the official website. The company logo came up on the screen. It was a dark blue circle made up of the letters 'G' and 'S'. Then the home page appeared with links to other divisions of the company – GS Automobiles, GS Homes, GS Telecoms, GS Air, GS Records, GS Solutions – each one had the same logo.

She went back to the search results and found a recent newspaper article with a picture of a silver-haired man next to it.

Multi-billionaire Brant Buchanan has had another run-in with animal activists, who have accused his company, Global Sands, of engaging in cruel animal experimentation without proper regulation.

Buchanan, founder of Global Sands, the worldwide corporation with an annual turnover of over £10 billion, dismissed the allegations as 'ill informed'.

The animal activists have threatened legal action but they have quite a fight on their hands. Famed for his ruthless business tactics, Buchanan is generally acknowledged to be one of the most powerful men in the world.

Holly flicked through some of the other articles. There were lots of boring business pieces on Buchanan's plan to buy a major insurance company, but Holly was more interested in reading about allegations of animal cruelty. She followed links to animal–activist sites speculating on what experiments Global Sands was involved in. It was horrible. She saw pictures of monkeys and rabbits in laboratories, dissected rats and mice. Willow miaowed at Holly's ankle, and Holly picked her up.

A motor engine stopped outside the house. She looked through the window and saw an extremely expensive silver car. The driver, dressed entirely in grey, leapt out and opened the back door in one smooth movement. A silver-haired man in a black suit emerged from the car and walked towards Holly's front door.

The doorbell rang. She looked back at the pictures on the computer screen. She could hear Big Hair answer the front door and her dad say, 'Mr Buchanan, it's such a great pleasure. Please come in.'

'Thank you,' replied a soft voice. 'Please call me Brant.'

Chapter Five

Downstairs, Big Hair was laughing loudly and saying, 'Tell me, Brant, do you really own three islands?'

'Four, actually. It sounds impressive but if you could see them, they're just lumps of rock really.'

Big Hair laughed loudly. Holly could think of nothing worse than joining them, but the food smells proved too tempting for Willow. She wriggled out of Holly's arms and ran downstairs.

'Willow,' whispered Holly. 'Willow.'

The cat ignored her, disappearing into the front room.

'Get away, you awful feline,' squawked Big Hair.

Holly darted down the stairs, into the room after

her. 'Leave her alone,' she said.

Big Hair was shooing Willow away with her foot. Dad was sitting next to her on the sofa. Opposite was Mr Buchanan. Up close, he was older than in the photograph on the website, his hair was more silver, his forehead more lined. And the picture hadn't done justice to his penetrating grey-green eyes, which descended upon Holly. She felt herself take a step backwards, as though his gaze was too intense to stand so close. She knocked a table behind her. A wine glass fell and smashed on the wooden floor. Willow jumped out of the way of the broken glass.

'I must apologise, Mr Buchanan,' said Big Hair. 'The creature isn't house-trained.'

Holly didn't know whether she was referring to Willow or her. 'I'm sorry,' she said, kneeling down to pick up the shards.

'Leave it,' barked her dad.

'Yes, get away,' said Big Hair, grabbing her hand, causing the sharp piece of glass that Holly had been carefully holding with her fingertips to slip. The edge was so fine that Holly didn't feel it cut into her skin, but a red slash appeared across her palm.

'Holly, you've cut yourself,' said her dad, sounding concerned.

'Look what you've done now,' scolded Big Hair.

Mr Buchanan, who had been watching with an air of detachment, seemed to get interested at the sight of blood. He leant forward. 'That will take some time to heal,' he said eagerly.

The fine red line thickened as blood oozed out. The sight of it made Holly feel faint. The pain was beginning to register.

'Don't drip on the furniture,' squawked Big Hair, grabbing a bowl from the sideboard and handing it to Holly. 'Hold this under it.'

Holly took the bowl in time to catch the first splash of blood.

'Does it hurt?' Mr Buchanan asked Holly.

'A little, yes,' she replied.

'Pain helps us understand our limits. Only by experiencing such extremes can we learn more about ourselves.'

'Is that why you hurt innocent animals?' said Holly angrily.

Mr Buchanan smiled and picked up Willow, who was purring by his feet. 'I believe animals are far more intelligent than we give them credit for,' he said. 'See your cat, for instance. She didn't cut herself on the broken glass.'

'Holly, follow me to the kitchen,' said Big Hair. 'Mind you don't drip on the floor on the way. And apologise to Mr Buchanan.'

'There's no need,' said the billionaire. 'I require a moment alone with your husband anyway.'

In the kitchen, Big Hair found the first-aid kit and bound Holly's hand roughly. The cut was bleeding quite a lot and any responsible parent would have rushed her straight to hospital but, for once, Holly was glad of the neglect, knowing that the wound would heal in her sleep. Self-healing skin was another of the dragon powers she had gained from Dirk's green blood.

'Now, stay out of trouble,' said Big Hair. 'This could make a big difference to us.'

'Dad shouldn't work for a man who hurts animals,' said Holly stubbornly.

'Your father needs to work,' she replied.

Big Hair busied herself in the kitchen. Holly went into the hall. She could hear the low murmuring from the front room. She wondered what they were talking about.

Still holding Willow in her arms she crept back to the door and, ever so gently, eased it open. She dropped Willow, who trotted into the room.

Using the door as cover, Holly slid in after her,

pushed herself against the wall and vanished from sight, turning exactly the same floral pattern as the wallpaper.

Dad shut the door and joined Mr Buchanan at the table.

'It's just the cat,' he said.

'She's persistent, I'll give her that,' said Mr Buchanan, feeding a mini fishcake to Willow. 'What's her name?'

'Err . . .' Her dad thought for a moment. 'Pillow? Something like that. She's my daughter's really. It's company for her, you know.'

'Children need company,' replied Mr Buchanan, scooping up Willow and carrying her to the door. 'She's very strong-willed, isn't she?'

'The cat?'

'Your daughter.'

'Oh yes. She takes after her mother.'

Holly concentrated hard on remaining still. She had never heard her dad say this before. As Mr Buchanan opened the door to let Willow out, his eyes flickered to the patch of wall where she was hiding. She closed her eyes. She heard him drop Willow in the hall and shut the door again.

'Anyway, back to the matter in hand,' said Mr Buchanan.

Holly opened one eye to see him walk back across the room, but he didn't sit down. Instead he put his palms outstretched on the table and leant over her father.

'Can you help me, Malcolm?' he said, fixing him with a firm gaze.

'I'm sorry. I honestly can't see how I can. I lost my job. The other lot deal with it now.'

'Yes, but we both know how these things work. Little will have changed. They haven't scrapped the AOG project. All I need is the location.'

Holly felt her heartbeat quicken. The AOG project was a secret government scheme. AOG stood for Acts of God and referred to weapons designed to create natural disasters. She knew this because she had helped Dirk Dilly stop a rebel group of dragons known as the Kinghorns from using an earthquake creator called the QC3000 from being stolen and used to wipe out half of Europe.

'No one will get hurt?' asked her dad nervously.

'Not one person,' replied Mr Buchanan.

'And my future will be secure?'

'Your future at Global Sands will be both secure and bright. Above all we reward loyalty.'

'Can I think about it?'

Mr Buchanan turned and took a couple of steps towards the door. Holly saw him bite his lip in frustration before putting on a smile and turning around.

'Of course you can,' he said, 'but please remember I have spoken to you in confidence.'

'Yes, I understand and I am grateful. I know how valuable your time is.'

'Valuable and expensive,' replied Mr Buchanan, inspecting another mini fishcake before thinking better of it and placing it back on the tray.

'Should I call you?' asked Mr Bigsby.

'No, I'll call you tomorrow. Please, don't disappoint me, Malcolm.'

Holly shut her eye again as Mr Buchanan opened the door and both men passed her. She heard Mr Buchanan thank Big Hair for the delicious food and leave.

Dad and Big Hair came back into the room.

'Well? What did he say? Did he offer you a position?' she asked.

'Yes.'

'That's excellent,' she squealed. 'You've accepted, of course.'

'I've said I'll think about it.'

'What's to think about? Oh, I see, you don't want to

seem too keen; make it seem like you've got other offers to consider. Very clever. You'll accept it, of course. Don't leave it too long; I don't think Mr Buchanan is used to waiting for anything. That's such good news. Now you'll have a decent income again we can get that new carpet.'

She picked up the tray of food and took it to the kitchen. Holly's dad followed her in.

Holly reappeared and ran upstairs to the phone on the landing. She picked up the receiver and dialled Dirk's number.

Chapter Six

Dirk yanked the television plug out of the socket with his tail. The rock band stopped rocking, the banging from next door stopped banging, Mrs Klingerflim stopped shouting and Alba stopped screaming. He picked up the ringing phone.

'The Dragon Detective Agency,' he said, catching his breath. 'Dirk Dilly speaking. How can I help you?'

'It's me . . .'

It was Holly's voice, but he couldn't hear what she said next because Alba spoke over her, saying, 'I have been telling you, already. I want you to help finding my sister.'

'I'm not speaking to you,' said Dirk to Alba, causing

the Sea Dragon to lower her head apologetically.

'What have I done?' said Holly, thinking he meant her.

'Not you,' replied Dirk.

'Then you will help me?' said Alba.

'Dirk, I need your help,' said Holly.

'No, I won't help you,' replied Dirk, again speaking to Alba.

'Why? What's wrong?' said Holly.

'You are very indecisive,' said Alba.

'Look, can I call you back?' he said into the phone, turning away from Alba.

'What's going on?' asked Holly.

'Why do you want to call me Back?' asked Alba. 'My name is Alba.'

'Nothing. I'll call you back,' said Dirk, hanging up.

'OK, I let you call me Back if you promise to help me,' said the Sea Dragon.

'Haven't you ever heard of a phone?' asked Dirk.

'Afone?' repeated Alba. 'I have not heard of Afone. Is this another of your crunchy-shelled humano foodstuffs?'

'Never mind. You have to go,' said Dirk, picking up the broken TV and placing it back on the filing

44

cabinet. 'You've caused enough damage for one day.'

'But I will not go without you,' she replied. 'I need your help. I need the help of the great Mr Dirk Dilly, dragon detective.'

'How do you know about me anyway?' asked Dirk, turning on her. 'How do you know where I live?'

'The Shade-Hugger said not to say . . . oops,' she said, clasping a paw to her mouth.

'What Shade . . .' Dirk stopped mid-sentence. 'Karny.'

'Captain Karnataka,' corrected Alba.

Dirk sighed. His old friend Karnataka was the most corrupt dragon he had ever met. He was a swindler, a con-artist and a thief. His most daring feat had been to steal the Council's Welsh gold reserves from under their noses, so it was ironic that the Council had since seen fit to elect him Captain of Dragnet, the dragon police force. At least his appointment was a marginal improvement on the previous captains, the yellow-backed Scavenger brothers, Leon and Mali, whose real allegiances lay with the mysterious Kinghorn leader, Vainclaw Grandin.

The question that bothered Dirk right now was why Karnataka would pass on his details to this Sea Dragon.

'I can't help you,' he said. 'I've already got a case on the go.'

'But if I do not find my sister, I do not know what I will do . . .' Alba broke off and burst into a howling wail.

The banging from next door started again.

'Oi, stop that bleeding racket, before I come round and give you an extreme close-up of my fist,' yelled the neighbour.

'Mr Dilly, the neighbours are complaining again,' shouted Mrs Klingerflim.

'All right,' Dirk said through gritted teeth. 'I don't seem to have any choice but to help you.'

Alba stopped making the noise.

'Are you talking to Afone or me?'

'You.'

'So you will help me find my sister?'

'Yes,' said Dirk, thinking that of all the bad ideas he had had in his life, this was the worst. Worse even than the time he decided to mix his favourite foods together, only to discover that the cocktail of orange squash, baked beans and toothpaste made him so violently sick that he set light to the carpet.

'Thank you. Thank you, Mr Dirk. I know you'll be able to find Delfina,' exclaimed Alba, hugging him.

Dirk staggered back, slipped on a plastic orange-squash bottle, and they both crashed to the floor.

'Is everything all right?' asked Mrs Klingerflim.

'Fine, Mrs K,' shouted Dirk, pushing Alba off. 'Get off me,' he growled.

'When do we start?' she asked.

'No time like the present.' Dirk scribbled a note for Mrs K and opened the window. 'Where were you supposed to be meeting your sister?'

'In Spain, where she is living.'

'OK, follow me.' He checked the street below and leapt out of the window to the roof across the road. Alba followed.

'Stay close,' he said, jumping to the next building. 'Do as I do. Don't let anyone see you.'

'I am as quiet as the dormouses from now on,' replied Alba, stepping on a loose tile and sending it sliding off the roof, smashing on the pavement.

'Come on,' said Dirk.

'Which way?' asked Alba.

'Up,' said Dirk, flapping his wings, taking to the sky.

Flying was risky but there was less danger of being seen at night, and Dirk was keen to get Alba out of London as soon as possible.

In fact, of the seven and a half million people in

London who could have looked up at that precise moment, the only person who did was an overweight advertising executive who, at the time, was lying on a park bench wearing a tracksuit, panting heavily. His wife had ordered him to give up chips and ice cream and take up jogging instead but, halfway round the park, he had collapsed on to the bench, exhausted and starving. Seeing the two dragon-shaped shadows in the sky he decided it must have been a side-effect of all this physical exertion, so he got off the bench and walked home, via the chip shop.

'It looks prettier from up here,' exclaimed Alba.

Dirk looked down at the twinkling lights of the city. London was at its best at night, with all of its ugly bits hidden by darkness. It reminded him that for all the bad human traits that his job brought him into contact with – the lying, betrayal, mistrust and deceit – what really made London remarkable was so many humans wanting to live in the same place. Dragons weren't like that. They lived lonely lives in remote places. They didn't have friends and they rarely stayed in touch with their families. Alba's concern over her sister wasn't typical. Dragons were abandoned by their mothers at an early age and often lost contact with their siblings altogether. It wasn't in their nature to look after each other, like it was with humans. Dirk had no family. Even if his mother hadn't been killed many years ago he was unlikely to have ever seen her again.

'I have heard some things about this humano settlement you live in. What is the Big Bean?' asked Alba, looking down.

'Big Ben,' corrected Dirk, pointing it out.

'And which is the Towel of London?'

'The *Tower* of London is over there,' he answered patiently.

'And where is a place called Old Ford Street?'

'You mean Oxford Street, and do I look like a tour guide? Enough questions,' snapped Dirk, flying into a thick layer of cloud.

For a moment they were in utter darkness, then they broke through the top into the clear night sky. The stars seemed brighter than usual and the moonlight painted the top of the clouds white, making them look like a luxurious quilt.

'Where exactly in Spain were you supposed to be meeting your sister?' asked Dirk.

'In the mountains, the Picos de Europa.'

'Then that's where we'll start looking for her.'

'But I am already telling you. She is not there.'

'Listen, Alba, if you want my help you'll do as I tell you, OK?'

'You are the boss, Mr Dirk,' she replied.

'Just Dirk,' he snarled. 'And yes, I am the boss.'

Chapter Seven

For several hours Dirk and Alba headed south, above the clouds, occasionally ducking or swerving to avoid aeroplanes. As they flew over the English Channel and Europe, Alba spoke incessantly but, to Dirk's relief the rushing wind carried her words away unheard. Dirk thought about Holly, remembering his promise to call her back. He felt bad. She had sounded like she needed his help. He resolved to call her as soon as he got the chance.

He hadn't flown so far in years and soon his wings grew tired. Instead of flapping them he tried catching rising air currents, which felt warm against his soft green underbelly.

Eventually, with the sun rising, and the sky growing lighter, Alba announced, 'She lives down here.'

Dirk flew down into the thinner part of the cloud. Below him was a rugged mountainous landscape where a cable-car ride took tourists up the rock face to take photos of the spectacular view. Luckily, being so early in the morning there were no tourists to take pictures of the two dragons swooping down from the sky.

Dirk and Alba landed on a mountainside by a stream. Dirk breathed in the thin early morning air. It felt fresh and cool. He surveyed the limestone valley. Living in London it was easy to forget that the world wasn't entirely crawling with human beings. Humans crammed themselves into the smallest of spaces, huddled together like scared animals, leaving vast areas like this uninhabited.

Alba pointed at a cave, halfway up a rock face, impossible to reach by foot. 'That is where she lives.'

'What's a Sea Dragon doing making her home so far from the sea?' asked Dirk.

Alba looked down, embarrassed. 'Delfina is . . .' she started. 'She's never been happy in the water . . . she was never a good swimmer . . .'

'Are you trying to say that she's a hard-back?'

Alba nodded sheepishly.

A hard-back was what Sea Dragons called other Sea Dragons who were scared of the water and whose backs had hardened after too much time on land. A few days back in the water and the skin would soften again, but their fear of water prevented them from returning to the ocean. Having a hard-back in the family was considered very shameful amongst other Sea Dragons.

Personally, Dirk had never seen what the big problem was. He was a Mountain Dragon but he hadn't lived anywhere near a mountain for years. His ability to blend was supposed to enable him to hide in the expansive mountainous landscapes, not the rooftops of London, but he had chosen the city life just as Alba's sister had chosen to shun the sea.

Alba spread her wings and flew to the cave, followed closely by Dirk.

The cave was larger than it had appeared from the valley. It was damp and shadowy. Dirk opened his mouth and breathed fire. His flame caught a pile of branches in the corner, setting them alight and filling the cave with flickering orange light.

'You see, Mr Dirk, she is not here,' said Alba. 'She has gone.'

'What's this?' said Dirk, looking at a line of grey powder on the cave floor.

'I do not know,' said Alba.

He licked his finger and dabbed it, inspecting it closely. 'It's ash,' he announced.

There was a line of ash around the cave. Dirk followed it like a dog following scent.

'What does it mean?'

The trail led him back to where he had started, as though the outline of ash formed an uneven circle. Then it hit him. He stood up on his hind legs and pushed Alba back.

'It can't be,' he muttered.

'Cannot it be what?' said Alba.

The ash had been smudged by their footprints, but the shape was still clear. The head. The wings. The tail. It was the outline of a dragon

'But no one has seen this in hundreds of year,' said Dirk.

'Seen what this?' asked Alba. 'What is it all meaning?'

'A Sky Dragon has materialised here,' said Dirk.

Chapter Eight

It was the first Saturday of the summer holiday and, after weeks of gazing out of stuffy classrooms at glorious sunny days, the sky was grey with the promise of rain. As Holly got off the bus the sky kept its promise and large droplets began to fall.

Last month, a few days before the general election, Holly had turned twelve. Predictably both her dad and his wife forgot all about her birthday. To punish them, she had unplugged the phone. Big Hair was furious because they had been expecting an important call, but Holly remembered Dad saying that when he called home he thought no one was in because it rang and rang without being answered.

She wondered whether Dirk might have accidentally done the same and kicked his phone lead out of the socket. He hadn't called back and when she tried calling him his phone rang out. She had resolved to go and visit him instead.

She pressed Mrs Klingerflim's doorbell. While waiting for the old lady to come to the door, she examined her palm. There was no sign of last night's cut.

'Who is it?' called Mrs Klingerflim.

'It's me, Holly.'

There was a pause as Mrs Klingerflim fiddled with the countless locks on the door. Eventually, the door opened and her owl-like face appeared. She smiled. 'Hello, dear. Nice weather for ducks.'

'Yes.' Holly stepped inside.

'Mind you, my Ivor used to say that just because ducks like sitting on water, doesn't mean they like it falling on their heads.' She laughed. 'He'd say, "I like sitting on comfy chairs, but I wouldn't want to get caught in a sofa storm."'

'His umbrella would break.' Holly added the punchline, having heard the story a number of times. 'Is Dirk in?'

'I don't know, do you want to go and have a look? He was making a terrible racket last night. The

56

neighbours were complaining.'

Holly took the stairs two at a time and knocked on Dirk's office door. There was no reply, so she entered his office. It was a tip. Dirk didn't have the highest cleaning standards at the best of times but this was more than the usual mess. She noticed the smashed television screen.

Mrs Klingerflim followed her in. 'Oh dear,' she said.

The rain was coming down so hard outside that it was splashing through the open window, dampening the carpet. Holly closed it. The traffic noises cut out, making the room seem suddenly quiet.

'I wonder where he's gone,' she said, tidying up the bits of paper from the floor and shifting them into a pile in the corner. She picked up what looked like a black paperweight, then noticed the book. It was red with a white zigzagged line across the front. She opened it up and read the title.

DRAGONLORE
A Scientific Study of Dragons
By Ivor Klingerflim

Dirk had told her about the book, but he hadn't let her look at it, telling her that she knew too much as it was.

Holly flicked through the pages. They were illus-trated with line drawings. She turned to the chapter on Tree Dragons and shuddered at the memory of the ones who had almost killed her at Little Hope Village Hall.

'How long did it take Ivor to write?' she asked.

'His whole life,' replied Mrs Klingerflim, taking the book from Holly and looking at it fondly. 'Dragon-spotting requires a great deal of patience. Some people think fishing is boring. It's got nothing on dragon-spotting. Ivor would spend every spare moment camp-ing out in some remote spot. When the children were grown up I'd go with him. Sometimes we would come home after a month having seen nothing. But when you did see one, even just a glimpse, it made it all worthwhile. When you have seen the Desert Dragons of California at dusk . . . well.'

Mrs Klingerflim stopped to wipe a tear from her eye. She shut the book.

'Mrs Klingerflim, do you remember when I first came here and said I was Dirk's niece?'

'That's right. What a dreadful fib,' said the old lady.

'But if you knew Dirk was a dragon, then you knew I was lying. Why did you let me in?'

'Ah, well. Dragons aren't the most sociable of

creatures, are they? They don't need friends and family like we do. But do you know, since Mr Dilly has been living amongst us I think he's picked up some of our habits. In a funny way, he's become a bit more human. So I thought he needed a friend, and when you arrived and since you were so clever to track him down, I decided maybe you would make a good friend for him. Oh, look, a note.' Mrs Klingerflim picked up a piece of paper on the desk. She stretched her arm out straight to read it. 'It's no good,' she said. 'The writing's too small for my old eyes. What does it say?'

Holly took the note and read it out loud.

Mrs K
Away on case for few days. Will pay rent when get back,
Dirk
PS Sorry about mess

'Ah, mystery solved.'

There was an awkward pause while Holly tried not to feel disappointed that he hadn't mentioned her in the note.

The silence was broken by the doorbell.

'I wonder who that could be?' said Mrs K, heading down the stairs.

Holly put the note back on the desk. She pushed open the window and looked down. There were two men standing on the doorstep; a tall one with a strand of wet hair combed over his head, and a shorter one, whose curly red hair was made even curlier by the rainfall. The tall man took a step back and Holly saw his face.

She ducked back inside and shouted, 'No, Mrs Klingerflim. Don't answer it.'

She ran to the landing but it was too late. Mrs Klingerflim was already opening the door and saying, 'What can I do for you two gentlemen?'

'Ah, yes, please allow me to introduce myself. My name is Arthur Holt and this stocky gentleman is my friend and colleague, Mr Reginald Norman. We are two small-scale philanthropists, looking for ways to help the situation of the neighbourhood's elderly and infirm, vis-à-vis, a non-profit-making all-encompassing service provider.'

'We're odd-job men,' added the other.

Chapter Nine

The last time Holly had encountered Arthur and Reg, the two crooks were working for the mysterious Vainclaw Grandin, unaware that their boss was in fact a dragon who wanted to conquer and enslave their entire species.

'Well, my guttering needs looking at. Are you pricey?' said Mrs Klingerflim.

'Our services are offered for entirely magnanimous reasons,' said Arthur.

'That means we don't charge,' added Reg.

'I'm sorry, did you say you don't charge?' asked Mrs Klingerflim.

Holly tugged her sleeve. 'You can't trust them,' she

said in her ear.

'What a charming little girl,' said Arthur, smiling at her. 'Is this your granddaughter?'

'No one does odd jobs for free,' said Holly. 'It doesn't make sense.'

'Your scepticism is misplaced but not entirely without precedence.'

'Oh yeah,' agreed Reg, nodding. 'They all think we're animal crackers when we tell them, but it's true. It's something to do with utensils.'

'What my cuddly companion is trying to say is that Reginald and I are foot soldiers of utilitarianism,' said Arthur.

'That's the word . . . You–tell–an–aerial–person?' ventured Reg.

'U–tili–tar–ian–ism,' repeated Arthur. 'It's a simple philosophy summed up in the sentiment: *the greatest happiness for the greatest number of people.*'

'Don't listen. It's a trick,' whispered Holly.

'My companion and I are trying to give something back to society.'

'Not that we've taken nothing,' said Reg quickly.

Arthur shook his head solemnly. 'Oh, Reginald, let us not forget that we have walked in the valley of darkness. We have on occasion stumbled on to the

62

wrong side of the law. But now we are reborn, reformed and at your service.'

'Are you selling something?' said the old lady.

Arthur laughed. 'We are but two men standing in front of one elderly lady asking her if there are any odd jobs that need doing.'

'We don't want anything from you,' said Holly out loud.

'Fair enough,' said Arthur, backing away. 'We understand. Have a good day, the both of you.'

'And be 'appy,' added Reg.

Mrs Klingerflim closed the door. 'What a funny to-do,' she said.

'I need to go,' stated Holly.

'Already? You've only just got here.'

'Sorry, I've just remembered I need to be somewhere,' she said, thinking it best not to tell Mrs Klingerflim that she was actually off to follow the two crooks.

'Why don't you hang on to this?' said Mrs K, handing her the red book with the white zigzag across the front. 'I think you'll find it quite interesting. Don't lose it, mind. It's my only copy.'

'Thanks, I'll look after it.' Holly slipped the book into her coat pocket, hugged Mrs Klingerflim and left.

The rain had eased off. Arthur and Reg were on the opposite side of the road, knocking on a door. An elderly man answered. Holly couldn't hear what they were saying but it looked like they were giving him the same routine. The old man must have bought it because he invited them in. Holly checked for traffic then crossed the road. Along the side of the house was a path where the residents kept their wheelie bins. The first gate on the right led to the old man's backyard. Holly headed down the path. She heard the back door open and Arthur's voice say, 'Yes, we are foot soldiers of utilitarianism.'

She peaked through a gap in the wooden fence and saw the crooks walk into the backyard.

'Well, it's very kind of you to help. I'd have done it myself but a rather nasty hiccupping episode last week brought back an old war wound.'

'You were in the war? How interesting,' said Arthur. 'I bet you have lots of stories you'd like to regale us with. We'd love to hear them, wouldn't we, Reg?'

'If it would make you 'appy to tell us, yeah,' said Reg enthusiastically.

'How nice,' said the old man. 'People don't seem so interested in my stories these days. I'll show you my collection of antique weapons if you'd like.'

'We'd love to see them, as soon as we have cleared up these leaves for you,' said Arthur, smiling.

'You want them put in bags?' said Reg.

'Yes, please. Are you sure you don't want paying?'

'As long as it makes you 'appy, we're 'appy, ain't we, Arthur?'

Arthur nodded. 'Indeed. Reginald, I will take the burden of holding the bag, while you scoop up the leaves and place them within.'

'Right–oh,' said Reg.

Holly watched them work, while the old man stood in the doorway. 'Why did you say you were doing this, then?' he asked.

'We were once on the wrong side of the law, weren't we, Reg?' said Arthur.

'That's right. Rotten as a pair of bad bananas,' said Reg.

'And then we had an awakening.'

'It was like a miracle, weren't it, Arthur?'

'A miracle, indeed. I remember standing outside a train station somewhere, Stonegarth, I think it was called, when I felt a sharp slap on my cheek.'

'I 'ad the same thing,' added Reg.

'It was as though we awoke from a strange dream,' continued Arthur, 'with the clear knowledge that from then on our mission was to make the world a better place.'

'It brings a tear to my eye to think about it,' said Reg, 'and not just because of how hard the slap was.'

In an instant, Holly realised what had happened. The last time she had seen Arthur and Reg they had still been under the powerful hypnotic spell of Dirk's Dragonsong. She remembered how Dirk had leant forward and said something she couldn't hear. She realised he must have told them to give up crime and dedicate their lives to making the world a better place.

'Where do we put the bag?' asked Reg, tying it up and throwing it over his shoulder.

'Outside the gate, please,' replied the old man.

The ill-fitting gate rattled. Holly quickly pressed herself against the fence and imagined what it was like to be this varnished wooden fence. As the gate opened she turned the same dark wood colour, vanishing from sight. Reg dropped the bag outside and Holly heard a mobile phone ring.

'I think that's coming from you,' said the old man.

'Indeed, you seem to be correct,' said Arthur. 'I'd forgotten I even had a phone.'

'Maybe you shouldn't answer it. It might be one of our old mates, asking us to do some dodgy job,' said

Reg, sounding concerned.

'If it is indeed a member of the criminal community, a scallywag, a ne'er-do-well, a rogue, I shall inform them of our new path, the long and winding road to happiness.'

'Yeah, good idea,' sad Reg, pulling the gate shut behind him. All three men went back into the house.

Holly moved and her natural colour returned.

'So you *can* turn yourself invisible,' said an astonished voice.

She froze then looked behind her to see a boy with blue eyes and dirty blond hair, balanced on top of a fence, staring at her in disbelief. This was bad. Not only had she been seen using dragon magic, she had been seen by the worst possible person, Archie Snellgrove.

Chapter Ten

'Where are we go now? Are you believing a Sky Dragon has taken Delfina? Why would they be doing that? Have you ever seen one? I have never seen one. Not materialised, at least,' Alba said, barely taking a breath between each question, her yellow eyes blinking in the darkness.

Alba Longs was proving to be the most irritating dragon Dirk had ever met. In fact, she was proving to be the most irritating thing he had ever encountered. It wasn't just the incessant chatter. She had a habit of poking Dirk with her claw every time she said something. Dirk was doing his best to keep calm and resist the urge to SNAP HER CLAW RIGHT OFF!

A dark sphere of shifting rock surrounded them. Dirk had asked the rock in Dragonspeak to take them down to the massive network of underground tunnels, where thousands of dragons dwelt, far out of the reach of humans. They were heading for the lithosphere tunnel, the outermost arm of the matrix, which circled the globe and could be reached from any part of the world.

'We're going to see Karny,' said Dirk.

'Mr Captain Karnataka?' replied Alba. 'How can he be helping us? He was the one who sent me to you.'

'Karny always knows what's going on in the dragon world and now he's got thousands of Drakes answering to him he'll be even better informed. If the Skies are on the move he'll know about it.'

'I do not like those Drakes, horrible creatures,' spat Alba.

Dirk nodded in agreement. Drab-nosed Drakes were fireless, wingless dragons with floppy noses, big bellies and small brains. They went into the Dragnet for the power the black metal neck cuffs and chains gave them.

The rock beneath Dirk and Alba's claws pulled away and they plummeted into a large tunnel lit with the dim orange glow of earthlight.

Dirk stood up and dusted himself down. 'Now, if memory serves me correctly, Dragnet HQ is this way,' he said.

'I do not think the captain will be able to help us?'

'Me and Karny go back a long way,' said Dirk, walking down the tunnel. 'Besides, it's his fault I'm involved in this. I've still got a case open back in London. The sooner I can solve this one the better.'

'But you care why my sister has been vanished?'

'It's just another case to me,' shrugged Dirk, walking away. 'The first thing you learn as a detective is to never let it get personal. At the end of the day it's only a job.'

Behind him Alba let out a long wailing noise. 'Ahhh,' she cried.

'Don't be so melodramatic,' said Dirk, refusing to turn around.

'Get off me,' squealed Alba.

Dirk spun around to see Alba with a black metal cuff attached to her neck. He felt a sharp pain as an identical cuff snapped around his own neck.

'You is under arrest, boy,' said the dust-grey Drake with the chain attached to his short stumpy tail.

Dirk reared up on to his hind legs and roared fire, but the flames bounced off the Drake's armour-like skin. The Dragnet officer swung his tail down, dragging the chain, neck cuff and Dirk violently to the ground.

'Good work, Junior,' said the Drake holding Alba. 'That's it, use your tail. Show that traitor who's boss.'

With their long floppy noses and inflated bellies, Drakes looked almost comical, but Dirk knew well that once a Dragnet officer had a dragon cuffed, there was no way out. Iron or steel, Dirk could have bitten through, but Dragnet chains were made from black metal, forged in the liquid fires of the Outer Core. It was ten times stronger than any metal known to humans.

'You hold on tight now, Junior,' said the larger of the two Drakes.

'Sure thing, Pappy,' said the other, swinging his tail so that Dirk felt another painful jolt around his neck.

'You are hurt my skin,' complained Alba.

'On what grounds are you arresting us, Drake?' demanded Dirk, addressing the larger of the two.

'You speak to Pappy with respect,' said the other, smashing Dirk's head against the ground.

'Well done, Junior,' said Pappy. 'You'll make a fine Dragnet officer, just like your old pappy and my pappy before me. And his pappy, your great-grand pappy. And his pappy, your great-great-grand—'

'On what grounds?' interrupted Dirk, his head throbbing.

'Tell him, Junior,' said Pappy.

'We is arresting you on grounds that we is currently in a state of emergency as declared by our glorious captain, Karnataka the fearless.'

'Karnataka the fearless?' laughed Dirk. He had heard Karny described as a lot of things but never fearless. 'Why has Karny declared a state of emergency?'

'The Kinghorns are on the rise,' said Junior. 'There's talk that they're gathering an army, preparing for the big attack. Captain Karnataka has told us to arrest any dragon acting suspiciously and you two is definitely suspicious.'

'But we are just looking for my sister,' said Alba.

'Sounds mighty suspicious to me,' said Pappy. 'What do you think, Junior?'

'Mighty suspicious, Pappy.'

'We are not doing anything the wrong,' pleaded Alba.

'A Mountain and a Sea Dragon skulking down the western ring of the lithosphere tunnel during a state of emergency,' said Pappy. 'You two is sure-fire criminal types.'

'No, this is Mr Dirk Dilly,' said Alba. 'He is a famous detective. I am Alba Longs. Mr Dirk is helping me to find my sister.'

'Keep quiet, Alba,' snarled Dirk.

'Famous detective, eh?' said Pappy. 'Well, I'm a bit of a detective myself and I detect the blood of a couple of Kinghorns.'

Dirk sighed. He had learnt from previous experience that for all their self-importance, Dragnet officers were almost always looking for what they could get out of a situation. He was yet to meet one who couldn't be bribed.

'OK,' he said, 'what will it take to persuade you to let us go?'

Junior pulled hard on the chain, bringing Dirk's face close enough for him to whack it with his fat fist. 'You can't bribe Pappy,' he said. 'My pappy is the most honestest officer in Dragnet. He ain't never taken a backhander. Ain't that right, Pappy?'

'Er . . . sure thing, son,' said Pappy, although Dirk could see from the look on his face that if his son hadn't been there it would have been a different story.

'Rats,' muttered Dirk. 'Of all the Drakes in all the world we had to meet these two prize specimens.'

'What was that, Mountain Dragon?' said Pappy.

'I said, we'll come quietly,' he said out loud.

'You see, Junior. Now he's showing some respect. All these dragons understand is a firm cuff.'

The two Drakes set off down the tunnel, pulling Alba and Dirk behind them

'How can we find Delfina now?' said Alba.

'Never mind her,' replied Dirk. 'How are we going to get out of this?'

'Surely they will let us go when they realise we are innocent,' she said.

'You two Kinghorns keep quiet,' yelled Junior.

'You tell them no good traitors, Junior,' said Pappy.

'Oh yes,' said Dirk, under his breath. 'They seem like a very open-minded pair.'

Chapter Eleven

Holly had been concentrating too hard on following Arthur and Reg to check if anyone was following her. Archie had seen her vanish from sight then reappear. She could have kicked herself for being so careless but kicking herself wouldn't have helped, so, instead, she let her face relax into a smile and laughed.

'What are you talking about?' she said.

'Don't try and deny it,' said Archie, jumping down from the fence into the alleyway.

'Don't try and deny that I can turn invisible?' laughed Holly. 'OK, you're right, I can turn invisible. I thought everyone could. Can't you?'

'Course I can't. That's how you kept getting away

from me. How are you doing it?'

'I come from a long line of invisible people.' Holly chuckled.

'Listen, I know what I saw and I saw you turn invisible.' Archie was getting annoyed.

'Then go and tell someone. See if they believe you,' replied Holly.

'They will when I get evidence. I'm going to stick so close behind you you'll think I'm your shadow.'

'Yeah, you've done a great job of following me so far,' she said sarcastically. 'You don't even know where I live.'

'Yes I do. Elliot Drive. Number forty-three,' said Archie triumphantly. 'I looked you up in the phone book. Why are you following them two blokes?' he asked, standing in her way with his hands in his pockets.

'It's none of your business what I do. Haven't you got anything better to do than follow me about?'

Archie thought about this before replying, 'It's the summer holidays. What else is there to do?'

'Just leave me alone,' said Holly.

'Come on, we could follow them together,' said Archie.

'Why would I want you anywhere near me?' snapped Holly.

'It'll be easier with two of us.'

'I thought you hated me,' she said, thinking of all the names he had called her.

Archie looked at his feet. 'I didn't know you,' he said apologetically. 'I am sorry about being so horrible to you at school.'

'You were really vile, you know.'

'I know.' He looked her straight in the eye. 'I tell you what, when we go back to school after the summer you can call me names in front of everyone. Any names you want. And I won't say anything back. No, better than that. I'll agree with you, whatever you say.' Archie reached out a hand. 'Come on, let's be friends.'

Holly looked at his grubby fingernails. No one had ever asked to be her friend. The only real friend she had was Dirk. She had spent too long hating Archie to trust him, but weighing up the options she could see that it would be easier to pretend to be friends than keep him as an enemy. Besides, she liked the idea of humiliating him in front of all his friends.

'Any name I want and you'll agree?' she said.

'Yep,' replied Archie.

They shook on it then Archie rummaged in his coat pocket and pulled out a couple of jelly beans. 'Let's seal the deal with a jelly bean,' he said, offering one to Holly.

'Have they just been loose in your pocket?' she asked.

'Yep,' smiled Archie.

'No way,' she replied.

'Suit yourself.' He threw them both into his mouth. 'So you're going to tell me how you turn invisible?' he asked.

Dirk had once told her that the art of telling a good lie was to tell as much of the truth as possible and change only one or two key details.

Holly said, 'It's called blending and it's easy, you just have to stay very still and think like whatever it is you're trying to blend with.'

She left out the small detail of swallowing the blood of a Mountain Dragon first.

Alba was still pulling against the chain but Dirk had decided it was better to conserve his energy.

'Where are we taking them, Pappy?' asked Junior.

'When you is in the lithosphere tunnel, you ain't never too far from a lock-up,' replied Pappy.

The Drake stopped in front of a metallic door, lifted up his droopy nose, and pulled out from underneath it a large key made from the same black metal as the door. He slipped it into the keyhole.

'Watch your old pappy demonstrate how to get an unwilling prisoner like this Sea Dragon into a lock-up. I call this move, the swing'em, smash'em 'n' slam'em.'

He entered the cell, then, using the door as leverage, he pulled on the chain and swung Alba inside. She screamed. The Drake stamped on the chain, bringing her head smashing to the ground. While she was recovering, and with surprising agility, he undid the cuff, dived through the door and slammed it shut behind him.

'I want to be getting out,' cried Alba through the small barred window in the door.

'Now your turn, son,' said Pappy.

Before Dirk could say he would go willingly, he felt the sharp edge of the metal cuff dig into his neck as Junior copied his dad, swinging him into the cell, smashing his head against the ground and slamming the door shut behind him. Dirk rubbed his sore neck.

'Good boy,' Pappy congratulated Junior, locking the door and handing him the key. 'You stay here and guard the convicts while I go and alert the Petty Patrol Officer.'

'What will he do, Pappy?'

'He'll inform the Chief Area Patrol Officer, who will tell the local magistrate, who will bring up the matter with the Dragnet Regional Manager at the next bi-millennial meeting. The Regional Manager reports directly to Captain Karnataka.'

'Couldn't you just tell Captain Karnataka yourself?' interjected Dirk. 'I'm an old friend of his.'

Pappy turned to look at him. 'This is Dragnet procedure,' he sighed. 'Tell them why we have procedure, Junior.'

'Because procedure is all that stands between Dragnet order and dragon chaos,' replied his son.

'Very good. Now, I won't be too long. You keep this door shut tight.'

'Yes, Pappy.'

'Remember, dragons can be tricksy. No matter what they say to you, do not open this door.'

'Yes, Pappy.'

'That's my boy.'

Pappy waddled down the corridor.

'What are we to do now?' asked Alba.

'There's not much we can do,' replied Dirk. 'Black metal was used to build these cells. It runs through the rock. The only way out is through that locked door. And the thing about that locked door is that it's locked.'

'But you said Captain Karnataka was your friend. He will let us out.'

'You heard them. It could be months before news gets to Karny.'

'Years,' said a low voice, which made them both jump. It came from the back of the cell. 'I've been here for six hundred and twenty-two years, four months and three days and my case hasn't even got as far as the magistrate yet.'

Dirk turned around to see two eyes set in a black head. 'Who are you?' he demanded.

'I'll exchange my name for yours,' said the dragon, standing to reveal a yellow underbelly.

'The name's Dirk Dilly. This is Alba Longs. And if I'm not mistaken, you're a yellow-bellied, coal-black Cave Dweller,' said Dirk.

The dragon nodded. 'They call me Fairfax Nordstrum,' he said. 'Well, they used to call me that when anyone called me anything.' He spoke slowly, as though carefully considering every word before speaking it. 'I've counted the days of my imprisonment on the wall.'

Dirk saw that the cell wall was covered in small lines scratched into the rock.

'What did they put you in for?' he asked.

'That's the funny thing, I can't actually remember. When my trial comes up I won't know whether to plead guilty or innocent.' He smiled wryly. Yellow smoke drifted from his nose. 'And what brings you to my little home?'

'Mr Dilly is a detective,' Alba started. 'He is helping me to finding my sister. But in the cave where she is living Mr Dilly found an outline of ash and this means that a Sky Dragon materialised there and I always thought Sky Dragons were just stories but then we met two Drakes and they threw us in this cell and now we are being on the wrong side of a locked door and we still haven't found my sister. Ow!'

Dirk slapped Alba in the face with his tail. 'You talk too much,' he said.

'I can help you find your sister,' said Fairfax.

'You can?' Alba started. 'How? Do you know her? Have you seen her?'

'No, but I know where Sky Dragons go after materialising.'

'Where?' asked Dirk.

'I'll tell you if you help me,' he replied.

'Help you do what?'

'Get out,' spoke Fairfax. 'Get me out of this cell and I will tell you where you can find this Sky Dragon.'

Chapter Twelve

Junior was feeling mighty pleased with himself. When he graduated from the Dragnet Cadet Academy his teacher, Sergeant Golub, had described him as the worst pupil that the DCA had ever passed. He said Junior had come closer than any other student in the whole of Dragnet history to failing the painfully easy exams. He said Junior would make the worst officer the Dragnet had ever seen.

Well, Junior had proved him wrong. He had assisted his pappy in capturing two traitors and now he had the very important job of guarding the cell until Pappy got back. He puffed his chest out and imagined the look on Sergeant Golub's face when he told him.

Junior's thoughts were disturbed by a voice.

'But if we cannot be getting out we will not be able to attend the meeting of secrets.' It was the Sea Dragon inside the cell.

'You mean the secret meeting,' said the Mountain Dragon, 'when all the Kinghorns in the world will be meeting in one place?'

'That is what I am meaning, yes, the secret Kinghorn meeting.'

'Will you keep your voice down about the secret Kinghorn meeting?' hushed the other.

'What does it matter? We are stuck in this cell.'

'Someone might overhear.' The Mountain Dragon lowered his voice, but Junior put his ear to the door, so he could still hear. 'If that Dragnet officer out there overheard and if he was smart he would cook up a devious plan.'

What sort of plan? thought Junior.

'What sort of plan?' asked the Sea Dragon.

'He could unlock the door, wait for us to escape, then follow us to the secret location.'

Junior listened intently.

'Why would he do that?'

'Because then he could bring more officers there and arrest every single Kinghorn in one go,' said the male voice.

'Wow, that would be bad for us, but good for him. They would probably be giving him a medal,' said the female voice.

'They'd cover him in medals. So you'd better keep your voice down about the *you know what.*'

'You mean, the secret meeting of all the Kinghorns?'

'Exactly.'

Junior's mind was working overtime. This was big. Really big. Sergeant Golub would look pretty dumb when Junior was given a medal.

Pappy had told him to keep the door locked no matter what the traitors said to him, but they hadn't said anything *to* him. What they had said, he had overheard, and how could they trick him if they didn't know he was listening?

He lifted his nose and pulled out a key. He remembered how Sergeant Golub had said that he had no initiative. He would show him. He unlocked the door and crept back into the shadows.

It didn't take long for the door to open and the Mountain Dragon's head to appear.

'The door's open,' he said. 'Come on, the coast is clear.'

Junior held his paw to his mouth to stop himself from chuckling.

The door opened wider and the two dragons stepped out.

'Does this mean we can go to the secret meeting after all?' asked the Sea Dragon.

'Be quiet about the secret meeting,' scolded the Mountain Dragon. 'You never know who might be listening. Come on. Let's go.'

Junior removed the chain and cuff so that he could follow them without clinking. He was feeling extremely pleased with himself. On his end–of–term report, Sergeant Golub described him as 'stupider than an exceptionally, stupid small–brained sizzle lizard'. He would have to eat those words when Junior had caught all the Kinghorns.

The feeling of immense pride that was growing in his large belly suddenly vanished with a sharp pain that appeared in his head. A great force hit his back. He fell forward, landing on his face, pinned to the ground.

He saw the Mountain Dragon and Sea Dragon turn around.

'I order you to release me. I am an officer of Dragnet,' he protested.

He couldn't see the third dragon that had jumped on him from behind but he could feel its weight on his back and its claws dig into him.

'This is for all those years in that cell,' it whispered.

'Don't hurt him,' said the Mountain Dragon. 'Just bring him back to the cell.'

The first rule of being a Dragnet officer, Sergeant Golub had always said, was never lose your chain and cuff. Dragons were naturally stronger, faster and better equipped than Drakes, but the standard-issue black metal Dragnet chain and cuff enabled a Drake to control even the biggest, toughest dragon. He felt himself dragged to his feet and hauled backwards.

Junior assessed the situation. He was unarmed, outnumbered and outwitted. He struggled helplessly as the Mountain Dragon attached the cuff around his neck before swinging, smashing and slamming him into the cell. The situation was bad.

'You're being awful silly. Locking a Dragnet officer in a cell is against the law, you no good traitors,' he said, through the grate in the door.

'I'll leave you the key, then,' replied the Mountain Dragon, dropping it within sight, but out of reach. 'And don't call me silly,' he snarled.

Junior was depressed. He had been tricked. Maybe

Sergeant Golub was right, maybe he was the stupidest, most useless Dragnet officer on the force.

'Don't leave me here,' he begged.

'Your imprisonment will be a blink of an eyelid compared to mine,' said the black and yellow dragon bitterly.

'Yes, your old pappy will be back soon enough to let you out,' added Dirk.

Junior groaned. 'I don't want him to find me like this,' he said.

'We can't have you following us, can we now?' said Dirk, feeling a little sorry for the Drake.

'That is right,' said the Sea Dragon. 'We are going to the secret meeting.'

The three dragons turned around and walked away.

'You know there isn't a secret meeting, really, don't you, Alba?' said the Mountain Dragon.

'No secret meeting? Why did we . . . oh, I see. We were having a trick with him.'

The last thing Junior saw of them was the Mountain Dragon shaking his head in despair before the three dragons disappeared around a corner.

Chapter Thirteen

Upstairs on the bus home Archie spent the whole journey trying unsuccessfully to blend with the grubby chequered seat.

'You're not sitting still enough,' said Holly, smiling to herself.

'The bus is too bumpy,' complained Archie.

'Try it later, when you're at home.'

The thought of Archie spending hours on end, trying to think like a sofa, without moving a muscle, was sweet revenge for his horrible behaviour.

Holly pressed the bell and stood up. 'This is my stop,' she said, heading downstairs.

'Where are you going?' asked Archie, following her.

'I'm going home,' she replied.

The bus stopped and she got off.

'Can't I come with you?' pleaded Archie, jumping off after her.

'No, you can't.' Holly still had Mrs Klingerflim's book in her pocket. She wanted to get home and read it. 'You can come and call for me tomorrow if you want,' she suggested, striding off towards Elliot Drive.

'Can't I come round now?' asked Archie, catching up with her.

'What, so you can have some scones and caviar and feed the corgis?' said Holly pointedly.

'I am sorry about all that,' said Archie.

'Why were you so mean to me anyway?'

'You're different, is all. Everything's always the same around here. Nothing ever happens at Gristle Street. Nothing interesting, but you've been to loads of other schools. You've been to William Scrivener's,' Archie said, his eyes wide.

'You're not missing much, believe me,' replied Holly.

'Did you meet Petal Moses?'

'I was put in the same room as her.' Holly had hated every minute of her time incarcerated inside the celebrity school and it was made all the worse by

90

sharing a room with Petal Moses, the spoilt daughter of an international popstar.

'What was she like?'

'Awful.' Holly smiled. 'Her mum actually paid people to phone her up and tell her how brilliant she was.'

Archie laughed. 'What about the Prime Minister's son. Did you meet him?'

Holly nodded, but she didn't want to discuss crazy Callum Thackley. She had sent him two letters since she left the school. In his replies he sounded as mad as ever.

Archie had followed her all the way home and didn't look like he would take no for an answer, so Holly relented, saying, 'You can come in but only for a minute.'

As they approached her front door, she felt nervous. It was the first time in her whole life that she had brought a friend home.

The door swung open and her dad almost walked straight into them both.

He looked down. 'Oh, hello . . . er . . . Holly. You've got a friend,' he said, clearly surprised. He was dressed smartly in a suit and tie, holding a briefcase.

'Hi, Dad, this is Archie,' she said.

'Are you a politician?' asked Archie.

'Was a politician,' Mr Bigsby replied. 'I lost my seat.'

'You didn't lose it. It was taken from you,' said his big-haired wife, appearing behind him, brushing non-existent dust particles from his suit. 'Anyway, darling, you have a better job now.'

'What job?' demanded Holly.

Big Hair glanced at her. 'Your father has accepted a position at Global Sands, so don't delay him.'

'You've taken the job?' exclaimed Holly, aghast.

She couldn't be sure but she thought she saw guilt in her father's expression as he avoided eye contact with her and mumbled, 'Needs must, Holly. Needs must.'

'Are you sure you don't want to take the car?' said Big Hair.

'The bus is just as quick. And that way I can swot up on the way,' he replied, tapping his briefcase.

'It would look a lot more professional if you drove.'

'Stop flapping, Bridget, the bus is fine,' said Mr Bigsby firmly.

Holly could tell that Big Hair was put out by the way he said it but she pecked him on the cheek and said, 'Well, off you go, then. Knock them dead, darling.'

Holly's dad coughed uncomfortably, awkwardly

patted Holly on the head, and left.

Big Hair's gaze fell upon Archie. 'I'm Holly's step-mother,' she stated. 'I'm glad she's finally made a friend. She's such a lonely girl. Would you like to come in? You'll both have to stay out of the way, mind. I've got a man coming in to see about new carpets.'

'Actually, we're going out,' said Holly, turning around.

'Suit yourself. Don't be too late,' Big Hair called after her.

Archie caught up with her. 'Where are we going?' he asked.

'We're following my dad,' replied Holly.

Once the three dragons reached a safe distance from the cell, Dirk stopped and said to Fairfax Nordstrum, 'I kept my side of the bargain. Now it's your turn.'

They were standing in the dim orange glow of the lithosphere tunnel.

'First things first,' said Fairfax, turning to face him. 'I've been shut up in that cell a long time. I'd like to know what's changed since I've been away.'

'Listen, Cave Dweller, I'm sorry you've been out of the loop for a while, but all I care about is finding this

Sea Dragon's sister, so I can get back to work.'

'Your detective work, yes,' said the black and yellow dragon. 'That does sound fascinating. What sorts of things do you . . .' He paused to emphasise the word, '. . . detect?'

'It's none of your business,' Dirk growled, smoke billowing threateningly from both nostrils. 'We had a deal.'

'Calm yourself,' replied Fairfax casually. 'I have no intention of going back on it. I just want to know what's been going on during the last six hundred years.'

'Nothing's changed. Humans still roam the earth, dragons still hide, fish still swim, birds still fly, rock's still rock and I'm still I,' said Dirk. 'End of story.'

'That's rather poetic. And are the Kinghorns really on the rise again as those Drakes said?'

'I am hearing they are planning to start a war,' said Alba.

'A war?' replied Fairfax. 'How terrible. And who is leading them in this war?'

Alba lowered her voice. 'A Mountain Dragon called Vainclaw Grandin. They call him the first up-airer.'

'Enough,' said Dirk, whose only encounter with the Kinghorn leader had almost cut short his own life. 'If you don't tell us where to find the Sky Dragon, I'll open my mouth and blacken your yellow belly.'

'No need for threats. I said I would tell you and I will,' said Fairfax. 'As you know, all dragons get energy from the earthlight that emanates from the Inner Core.'

Dirk nodded. It was the earthlight which lit these tunnels far beneath the surface of the earth. It was as important to dragons as sunlight was to humans.

'Sky Dragons need it as much as we do,' continued Fairfax. 'But when they have spent a long time as gas, floating high, far from the source of their power, they are considerably weakened. After materialising they are exhausted. A small dose of sugar will revive them temporarily but what they really need is to recharge with earthlight energy.'

'So they come underground?' asked Dirk.

'Not just underground. When they materialise they need to build up their strength, so they go to the banks of the Outer Core, where they bathe in the liquid fire. It's painful but effective. A Sky Dragon at full strength is a powerful dragon indeed.'

'How do you know all this?' asked Dirk.

Fairfax's mouth curled into a smile. 'I have been around a long time. I've seen a lot of things. I remember a time when Sky Dragons roamed free, rather than hiding amongst the clouds. I've never heard of one kidnapping a Sea Dragon though.'

Dirk considered whether he had been rash in freeing Fairfax Nordstrum. There was something he didn't trust about the Cave Dweller.

'Where will you go now, Nordstrum?' he asked.

'I'll probably just go and find some quiet corner of the world to curl up in. I've been living on dirt for the last six hundred years. My needs aren't great. I just want somewhere quiet with fresh vegetation. The Andes, perhaps, or one of those little deserted islands off Scotland.'

'Good luck with that,' said Dirk.

Then, speaking in the ancient language of Dragonspeak, he asked the rock beneath his feet to take Alba and him down to the banks of the Outer Core. The rock, being rock, obliged unquestioningly and lowered the two dragons into the ground.

'And good luck with your detecting,' said Fairfax as they disappeared.

Chapter Fourteen

Archie and Holly hid behind a wall, watching Mr Bigsby wait at the bus stop.

'I can't believe you're following your dad now?' said Archie.

'You can leave any time you want,' replied Holly curtly.

'Do you always spend your Saturdays like this or is it because it's the holidays?' Archie chuckled, clearly enjoying himself.

'Shh,' hushed Holly. 'He might hear us.'

The bus arrived and Mr Bigsby waved wildly at it, as though worried it might not stop. As he got on he looked uncertain how to pay.

'I'm not sure he's ever been on a bus before,' said Holly.

'I knew you were posh.' Archie grinned, his hair falling over his brow.

'Come on,' she said.

They jumped over the wall and ran to the bus before the doors closed. Archie got on after her. Her dad had gone up to the top deck. They sat downstairs at the back.

'So, are you going to tell me why we're following your dad?' asked Archie.

'I don't trust the man he works for.'

'Why? Who's he work for?'

'Brant Buchanan. He's a billionaire. Dad only took the job because Big Hair kept going on at him.'

'You don't like your stepmum, do you?'

'She's not any kind of mum. She's just his big-haired wife,' replied Holly.

Archie grinned. 'She has got big hair. It's like a bird's nest.'

'A big bird's nest,' agreed Holly.

'Yeah, an ostrich's or an emu's. I wouldn't be surprised if there's an egg in there.'

Holly laughed and they spent the rest of the journey joking about what other wonders might lurk inside Big Hair's big hair. They were on the same bus that Holly and Archie took to school. When it passed Gristle Street Comp the empty school looked drabber and more rundown than ever. It felt strange not to get off at the usual stop. A few stops later Holly suddenly went quiet and ducked, dragging Archie behind the seat as well.

'He's getting off,' she whispered.

'Shouldn't we follow him?' he asked.

'Not yet. We need to keep our distance,' she said, waiting until the driver was shutting the doors before jumping up and shouting, 'Hold on, we're getting off.'

Waiting to cross the road, Mr Bigsby didn't notice his daughter and her friend dive behind the bus shelter. Instead, his attention was drawn by a small crowd of protesters standing on the opposite side, outside two large silver gates. The twenty or so protesters held placards with slogans that read:

ANIMALS HAVE RIGHTS TOO!

DUMB ANIMALS WORK FOR GLOBAL SANDS!

EXPERIMENT ON BRANT BUCHANAN
INSTEAD!

A couple of sturdy-looking policemen stood between them and the gates.

'This must be the lab I read about,' said Holly.

Her dad crossed the road at a zebra crossing. She waited until he was all the way across before following. He didn't go through the crowd, towards the silver gates, but walked straight past them instead. He stopped and looked around. Holly and Archie dived into the crowd to avoid being seen. One of the protestors had a loudhailer and was making a speech.

'. . . Brant Buchanan sits up there in his ivory tower. Well, I've got news for you, Mr Buchanan. Ivory is illegal in this country and when we knock down your tower you'll come tumbling down to earth.'

To Archie this sounded like a load of clever words that didn't really mean anything, but the other protestors seemed to enjoy it and cheered loudly, waving their placards in the air.

'Come on,' said Holly. 'He's gone round the side.'

At the corner she stopped and poked her head around.

'What's going on?' asked Archie.

'He's going through a back door,' she replied.

Holly turned the corner into a narrow alleyway. Set in the right side wall was a door. Archie moved to take a closer look, but Holly stopped him.

'There's a camera,' she said, pointing. 'They check who you are before opening it.'

Archie saw on the side of the door a panel with an intercom camera. 'So that's it. We can't go any further,' he said.

'I can,' replied Holly. 'But I need your help.'

Archie looked at her disbelievingly. 'Look, following people is one thing but breaking into a building is illegal.'

'But this is important,' replied Holly stubbornly.

'Why? Because you don't trust this billionaire bloke?'

'Look,' said Holly desperately, 'Dad used to be an MP. He worked for the Ministry of Defence. Now Brant Buchanan wants Dad to tell him the where-abouts of a secret weapon.'

'Brilliant!' Archie clapped his hands.

'So you'll help me?' said Holly hopefully.

'Holly, what you're talking about is called breaking and entering.'

'No it's not.'

'Yes it is,' exclaimed Archie angrily. 'I should know, my dad's in prison for it.'

Holly was stunned. 'Your dad's in prison?' she said.

'Yes.' The grin that lived on Archie's face disappeared.

'I'm sorry,' said Holly.

'I'm not. He's an idiot,' spat Archie.

Holly didn't know what to say. 'Maybe he'll have changed when he gets out,' she said.

'I don't think so. The last three times haven't stopped him,' he said bitterly. He pushed his dirty blond hair away from his eyes and stared defiantly at Holly.

Holly understood being angry with a parent. She had been angry with her dad ever since Mum had died. She had been angry at him when he married Big Hair so soon after her death. Every time he forgot her birthday or just gave her cash for Christmas she was angry at him. And now she was angry with him for accepting Brant Buchanan's offer.

'It isn't exactly breaking and entering,' she said at last. 'It's just entering.'

'If your dad is doing something dodgy, call the police.'

'The police don't arrest people like Brant Buchanan. They protect him. You saw them outside the gates, holding back the crowds,' said Holly.

'Look, Holly, I enjoy a good game as much as

anyone. Secret weapons and all, it's fun, but this isn't a game.'

Holly needed to persuade him to help her. She couldn't tell him the whole truth. He would never have believed her. But she remembered again the art of telling a good lie. Tell as much truth as possible, with one or two details altered.

'The truth is I work as a detective's assistant,' she said.

'What detective?' asked Archie, sounding sceptical.

'It's called the Dragon Detective Agency,' she replied.

'Cool name,' said Archie.

'It's my uncle's agency. His name's Dirk Dilly and he lets me help sometimes. That's how I know about the secret weapon. I know it sounds unbelievable but I swear it's true and I need to get into that building to find out what my dad's up to.'

Archie's smile returned to his face. 'Is that true? That's really cool,' he said.

'So you'll help me get in?' said Holly.

'Can I meet your uncle?'

'Yeah, I'll introduce you some time,' lied Holly.

'All right,' he said, at last, 'what's the plan?'

Holly told him what she had in mind and got into

position, along the wall by the door, out of view of the camera.

Archie watched as the colour drained from Holly's face and her whole body, including her clothes and shoes, turned the colour of the wall behind her, until all that was left were her brown eyes staring back at him.

He approached the door, pressed the buttons on the buzzer and pulled silly faces at the screen. Eventually the door opened and a burly uniformed security guard with a thick black moustache appeared.

'Get away,' he said.

'Can't I come in?' asked Archie.

'Noh a chance,' replied the security guard, in a thick Scottish accent.

'But I live here,' he protested.

'Right, and Ah'm Princess Margaret.'

'Your Majesty,' said Archie, bowing.

The security guard stepped forward threateningly. Archie saw Holly reappear and slip behind the man's legs.

'Ah'll set the dogs on you if you don't clear off,' said the large man.

'Sorry for wasting your time,' said Archie, turning around and walking away.

Chapter Fifteen

'I did not trust that Cave Dweller. He had a funny look. He had been locked away a long time. He cannot have spoken to anyone for many years. Imagine that, no one to talk to for all that time, just you and your thinking. Can you imagine it? Thinking this and that and that and this with no one to talk to?'

Dirk imagined it. It sounded nice. There was something about travelling by rock that made Alba talk incessantly.

'But onc thing I am not understanding,' she continued. 'If a Sky Dragon is so weak when it materialises, how could one be kidnapping my sister? Delfina is a strong dragon.'

'We don't know much about them,' replied Dirk. 'I've never seen one. Not in the flesh, at least. What bothers me is why a Sky Dragon would want to kidnap a Sea Dragon at all.'

'I cannot say, but I have heard that the Sky Dragons do not like other dragons. They think they are above us. Some say they can make a firewall. I have never seen what that is.'

While Alba whittered on, Dirk's mind wandered. He found himself thinking about Holly. He had got so wrapped up in this case that he had forgotten about her. He hoped she wasn't getting herself into too much trouble. He would make it up to her when he got back and take her for a trip over London.

As they neared their destination the pocket of shifting rock that surrounded them grew brighter and hotter, making Alba jumpy.

'This does not seem right to me. The banks of the Outer Core are only for pregnant dragons,' she said.

'And convicted criminals,' said Dirk, 'but they don't stop at the banks.'

Only a handful of dragons had ever been banished to the earth's Inner Core but of those who had, none had returned.

'What do you think it is like down there?' asked Alba.

'I can't imagine,' said Dirk, 'and I don't plan on finding out.'

Dirk thought about it. The blinding light and incessant heat would be unbearable.

'Do you think it is possible to be surviving down there?' asked Alba

'It's probably better if you can't,' said Dirk grimly.

Even this far down the air was stifling and Dirk had to squint at Alba in the dazzling earthlight.

'Brace yourself. I think we're there,' he said, feeling the rock pull away from under his feet.

They tumbled on to a stony shoreline. Dirk felt disorientated. It was an odd sensation, like he wasn't sure which way up he was. An acute burning feeling in his belly made him cry, 'Yee-ouch!' and jump to his feet. The scorching pebbles were painful on the tough skin of his feet but they had been agony on his soft green underbelly.

At the edge of the shoreline was an ocean of liquid fire, bubbling and popping like it had a life of its own. It seemed to go on for ever, steam rising up, obscuring the horizon.

'Welcome to the banks of the Outer Core, dudes.'

The greeting came from a Firedrake, sitting on the edge of the shore. Firedrakes were relatives of the drab-nosed Drakes and had the same large bellies and tough skin, but their noses were upturned and their backs were covered in tiny holes. This one wore what looked like a pair of crudely carved sunglasses and held a long black ladle. By his side were rows of black metal flasks. He dipped the ladle into the sizzling liquid, scooped some up and poured it into a flask. He then lifted it to his mouth, gulping it down greedily, licking his lips and burping, sending blasts of steam shooting from his mouth, nostrils and all the holes on his back.

'Wow, that tickles,' said the Firedrake, leaning back and laughing.

'I think this one is peculiar in the head,' said Alba, tapping the side of her head.

'Let's go say hello,' replied Dirk, approaching.

The Firedrake turned to look at them. 'Hey, dragon dudes, what's happening?'

'The name's Dirk Dilly,' he replied. 'Why are you drinking that stuff, Firedrake?'

'It's my job, dude . . . but I tell you what, after a while you develop a taste for it. The name's Shute.' The Firedrake extended a paw.

Dirk shook it. 'Shute?'

'Shute Hobcraft, Firedrake, at your service,' he said,

taking another sip of liquid fire, shooting out steam and bursting into hysterics.

'How can you drink something so hot?' said Alba.

'You wanna try some? I've got some vintage stuff here,' he said, holding up a flask. 'It really clears out your passages.'

'We're looking for a dragon,' said Dirk, already growing tired of the idiotic creature.

'There's one next to you,' giggled Shute, pointing at Alba.

'We're looking for a Sky Dragon,' said Dirk firmly.

'A Sky Dragon. Woo, dude. I haven't seen one of those for years.'

'Come on, Alba,' said Dirk. 'Let's check further along the bank.'

'There's no point,' said Shute. 'I can tell you, no Sky Dragon has been down this far in a long time.'

Dirk turned to face him. 'How can you be so sure?'

'I'll tell you if you have a swig,' he replied, holding out the flask, sniggering.

'I'm losing my patience,' said Dirk.

'Come on, I know you're going to like it,' insisted Shute.

'All right, just one,' said Dirk, taking the flask and looking warily at the bubbling liquid. He lifted it to his lips and took the tiniest of sips. The pain was immense. Dirk enjoyed a vegetarian vindaloo as much as the next dragon, but this was seriously scorching. Dragons needed fairly hardy insides to breathe fire but they didn't have the same kind of internal insulation as Firedrakes.

'Yeaahhhhhouch!' Dirk screamed out in agony.

Shute found this hilarious and fell about laughing. 'It's good, isn't it?'

'How can you be sure that no Sky Dragon has been this far down?' said Dirk in a measured tone.

'Because when any dragon goes into the liquid fire of the Outer Core the temperature drops, Sky Dragons, doubly so,' said Shute. 'My job is to test it. If it's one degree cooler I alert the authorities.'

'Why? asked Dirk.

'Because it probably means that a dragon has tried to escape the Inner Core. The bigger the dragon, the bigger the temperature drop. You should have tried it when Minertia went down. It was, like, coool, dude. She was one big dragon. The same would happen if a Sky Dragon took a dip.'

'You were here when Minertia was convicted thirty years ago?'

'Old Shute's been here for coming up to two

hundred years now. Still, I don't mind. As I say I've got to like the stuff,' said Shute taking another ladleful, pouring it into a flask and taking a swig. After reappearing from the cloud of steam in a fit of giggles, he said, 'All I know is that no Sky Dragon has been down here for a long time.'

'Thanks for your help,' said Dirk.

'No problem,' said Shute. 'Here, take one if you like.' He held up a flask with a top on.

'No thanks,' said Dirk, his mouth still burning.

Alba grabbed the flask and said, 'I will take it as a souvenir. Thank you.'

'Keep up the good work,' said Dirk, turning away.

'Hey, thanks, dragon,' said Shute. 'It's been a blast talking to you. Good luck finding that Sky Dragon.'

'I told you he was peculiar in the head,' said Alba, as they left.

'None of this makes sense,' said Dirk. He was beginning to feel frustrated.

'If only we knew more about the Sky Dragons,' said Alba.

Dirk looked at Alba. 'Great rats of Grimsby!' he exclaimed. 'That's it.'

'What is what?' she replied.

He didn't answer. He couldn't believe he hadn't

thought of it earlier. The book, *Dragonlore*. Ivor Klingerflim had written an entire chapter on Sky Dragons. He felt behind his wing but it wasn't there. He must have left it in his office, which meant one thing. He was going back to London.

Chapter Sixteen

Holly slipped behind the security man's large legs, through the doorway and pushed herself against the inside wall, turning the same colour white.

The security guard pulled the door shut and walked down the corridor.

Once he had gone round a corner, Holly reappeared and made her way cautiously in the opposite direction. She didn't know what her plan was, but she had to do something. She knew her dad wasn't a bad person. He wouldn't want to hurt anyone but she wondered whether he sometimes mixed up right and wrong.

She felt something brush against her leg and looked

down to see a tabby cat.

'Hello,' she said, bending down, but the cat ignored her and continued walking down the corridor.

Holly followed it, walking past a window that looked into a room full of cages with mice, cats and other animals inside. A door on the far side of the room opened and a young woman in a lab coat entered. She carried a plastic container with air holes in the top. Holly blended her head with the window, turning as transparent as the glass. The lab worker placed the container on the counter and opened one of the cages. A white mouse walked out of the cage into the container. The woman shut the cage door, picked up the container and left the room.

Holly continued down the corridor, ever prepared to stop, freeze and blend if necessary.

The cat passed a stairwell on the left then stepped through a cat flap in a door on the right. Holly stopped outside the door and looked through a pane of glass into a small room. The cat was sitting in a basket in the corner. By its side were two bowls, one of milk, another of cat food. The cat must have been very well fed, because it didn't seem at all interested in either bowl. Willow would have greedily emptied both bowls no matter how much she had already eaten.

Holly tried the door handle, half expecting it to be locked, but, to her surprise, the door opened. She entered the room, bent down and stroked the tabby. The cat made no response. It didn't purr or tilt its head so she could scratch it behind the ear, like Willow did. Nor did it flinch or move away. In fact, it showed no sign of noticing, let alone enjoying the attention.

Holly examined the collar around the cat's neck. It was metallic and reminded her of her dad's watch strap. She twisted it round and saw on the underside the letters G and S, formed into a circle: the Global Sands logo.

Behind her she heard an electronic whirring, a noise she recognised immediately. The last time she had heard that sound she had been planning an escape from William Scrivener School. She spun round to find a security camera pointing at her. She ran to the door and desperately tried the handle, but it was locked. She tried to find a blind spot, where she could vanish, but the camera followed her every move. She couldn't risk being seen blending. There was nowhere to hide. All she could do was sit and wait to get discovered.

'This is your fault,' she said to the cat, but the animal

remained perfectly still except for the gentle movement of its breathing.

When the door opened she looked up at the security guard. She recognised the black bushy moustache instantly. It was Hamish Fraser, the same guard she had encountered while trying to escape from William Scrivener's.

'It is you. Ah wasn't sure from the picture on the monitor,' he said in his familiar Scottish accent. 'What a wee world it is. What brings you here, Ah wonder?'

Holly thought fast. 'I came to find a toilet. I must have gone through a wrong door.'

'Nice try,' said Hamish, a grin spreading beneath his moustache. 'You accidentally stumbled into a maximum-security building looking for the lavvy? You'll have to do better than that, lassie.'

'Why aren't you at the school?' asked Holly.

'The school's shut for summer. Ah work here for a few months of the year. Ah'm on the late shift. Ah'm noh so keen on being locked up with all these wee animals, but thanks to you, it's already proving more exciting than I'd expected.'

'Where's Bruno?' asked Holly, remembering how Hamish had tried to train his poodle to be more aggressive.

'Bruno? In this place?' said Hamish, gesticulating towards the cat. 'He'd have a field day.'

'What's wrong with this cat?'

'Don't you worry about the cat, come on.' The security guard tightened his grip on Holly's shoulder and frogmarched her out.

'Can't you just let me go for old time's sake?' she pleaded.

Hamish laughed a loud throaty laugh and said, 'The last time Ah saw you Ah was trying to stop you breaking out. This time you've broken in. You're a right wee criminal in the making, aren't ye?' He led Holly up the stairs. At the top he said, 'In you go,' and pushed the door open.

The room she walked into was a stark contrast to the rest of the building. Instead of white walls and a tiled floor, it had dark grey walls and a plush green carpet. In front of her was a desk, made entirely from glass, behind which Brant Buchanan was sitting. At first she thought he was alone, but she turned to see, at the other end of the room, her dad sitting on a purple sofa, staring at her, his anger evident in his eyes.

'The irrepressible Holly Bigsby,' said Mr Buchanan, standing to greet her.

She avoided eye contact with her dad but could feel

his furious glare burning a hole in the back of her head.

'Your father is angry with you, but I am impressed,' said Mr Buchanan. 'When I designed his laboratory I knew that ill-informed animal activists and prying investigative journalists would try to get in. So there are no windows on the ground floor and these on the upper floor only open a couple of centimetres. Both entrances, front and back, are under constant surveillance. The roof is made out of a synthetic material too strong to be cut by any conventional tool. No one has ever got further than the silver gates without my say-so. Except you.'

Holly said nothing.

'What really annoys them, you see,' continued Mr Buchanan, 'is that for all their protests and leaflets and slogans, they have absolutely no idea what we do here. For all they know we're making marmalade.'

'You don't make marmalade,' interjected Holly. 'You experiment on animals.'

'Everyone experiments on animals,' said the billionaire dismissively. 'When NASA sends an astronaut into space or when a country sends a soldier off to war. When a politician tries out a new policy or a teacher tries a new lesson on his class. These are all animal experiments. Only, the animal is man. Why should our furry friends be excluded just because they can't sign a piece of paper?'

'I don't care how cleverly you say it, you're still hurting animals.'

'You're too young to understand,' said Mr Buchanan dismissively. 'Now, I need to check that you haven't taken anything from my laboratory. Empty your pockets.'

Holly did so, hoping he wouldn't notice the bulge in her coat pocket made by the book Mrs Klingerflim had given her.

'What's that?' he asked.

'It's just a book,' she replied casually.

'May I see it?'

'No.'

'Holly Bigsby,' boomed her father, finally breaking his silence. 'You have trespassed on Mr Buchanan's property, you have insulted him. I can't begin to tell you how . . . how disappointed I am in you. Do as you are told.'

Holly pulled out the book and handed it to Mr Buchanan across the desk. 'It's just a stupid book about dragons, anyway,' she muttered under her breath.

He took it, but his gaze remained on her open palm.

'Your hand has healed remarkably quickly,' he said.

'It wasn't that bad after all,' replied Holly, whipping it away quickly.

'Once again, I am sorry, Brant,' said Mr Bigsby.

'Not at all, Malcolm. Weaver will drive you back.'

Buchanan pressed a button and spoke through the intercom. 'Weaver, prepare the car, Mr Bigsby and his daughter will be exiting through the back door.'

'Can I have my book back?' said Holly, trying to sound casual, not wanting them to know how important it was.

'You'll get your book back when you've learnt your lesson,' replied her father.

'I'll hang on to it if you like, Malcolm,' offered Mr Buchanan, 'I've always had a soft spot for mythical creatures.'

He slipped it into the top drawer of his desk.

'Thank you,' said Mr Bigsby.

As the desk was made entirely of glass, Holly could see it easily enough but Buchanan locked the drawer and her dad took her hand and led her out of the room. She felt bad. She had promised Mrs Klingerflim she would look after it and now it had been confiscated.

Chapter Seventeen

Archie felt himself picked up by the armpits and hauled to the end of the alleyway. He looked up to see a man in a collarless grey suit, with jet-black hair that looked as though it had been sprayed on. The man must have moved very quickly and quietly to have snuck up on him like that without being heard.

Archie had been leaning against the wall outside the door, just out of sight of the camera, listening to the angry animal activists shouting slogans, eating jelly beans straight from his pocket, wondering how Holly was getting on.

Now he had got to know her he felt bad about all the horrible things he had said to her over the past few months. He had started calling her names because she was new and it made his friends laugh, and Archie lived to make people laugh. Holly seemed so immune to his teasing, that he thought it didn't bother her that much. If he had succeeded in following her home straight away he would probably have lost interest but, every time she lost him, it became more of a challenge.

'Oi, you can't go picking up people and moving them,' protested Archie.

The man didn't respond. He had his back to Archie, blocking the way to the alleyway.

The door opened and Holly appeared with her dad behind her. The grey man marched towards them. 'Mr Bigsby,' he said, 'I'm Weaver. The car is just up here.'

Holly's dad said, 'That's very kind. Thank you.'

'Is this child anything to do with you?' asked Weaver, indicating Archie.

'Hey, Archie,' said Holly miserably.

'Hey, Holly,' he responded cheerfully.

'Yes, I think we better take them both back home if that's all right, Mr Weaver,' replied Holly's dad.

'It's just Weaver,' said the strange man, pointing the keys at the car, unlocking it, and opening the back door.

'Wow!' said Archie.

'Wow!' said Holly.

Mr Bigsby didn't say anything, but it was obvious that he was thinking *wow!* too. Stepping into Brant Buchanan's Bentley was more like entering a top-of-the-range, high-tech, futuristic living room than getting into the back of a car. It had soft black leather seats, tinted windows, a plasma TV screen, a DVD player and rows of glowing red buttons along the doors, each one screaming out to be pressed. Weaver closed the door behind them and soft lighting came on.

'Don't touch anything,' said Mr Bigsby to Holly.

He was sitting facing backwards to keep his eye on her. Holly had never seen him look so angry. She wanted to tell him why she had followed him but she couldn't let on that she knew about the AOG Project. If she said anything that led to Dirk being discovered she would never forgive herself.

The plasma screen behind the driver's seat flickered to life and Weaver's unsmiling face appeared. He was sitting in the driver's seat. 'Could I take the young man's name, please?' he said.

'Archie Snellgrove,' said Archie, pulling the seatbelt chord. 'Why?'

'To find your address.'

'I'll walk back from Holly's house,' said Archie anxiously,

Weaver's face, which had been full-screen, shrunk into a small box in the corner. Archie's name appeared one letter at a time as though being typed out. The cursor flickered and a map of London appeared. A series of small flags sprung up. The picture zoomed in on south London, where a small red car was flashing. There was a flag nearby with an address on it.

'Number seventy-eight Sidney Clavel Estate,' read Weaver.

'How did you do that?' said Archie, impressed.

'If you would like a drink, the third button on your door is for orange juice,' said Weaver. As he started the car and set off, the little car icon on the screen moved towards the flag.

'Cool,' said Archie. He pressed one of the glowing red buttons and a panel opened next to the plasma screen.

'That's the photocopier,' Weaver said. 'You want the button above that one.'

Archie pressed another and instantly the armrest between Holly and him twisted around. The flat surface, which had been underneath, slid away to reveal a hole, out of which appeared a glass of orange juice.

'I told you not to touch anything,' said Mr Bigsby, leaning forward and taking the glass.

Classical music filled the car. With the gentle melody of the strings, the smooth running of the car and the tinted windows, it was as though they were gliding invisibly through the world. Holly wondered what it was like, always travelling like this, never having to fight your way on to crammed buses, and sit next to someone with a bottom so big that it took up both seats, or someone really smelly, or someone listening to rock music on their headphones so loudly you could sing along.

When the car arrived at Sidney Clavel Estate Holly understood why Archie thought she was posh. With flaky paint and crumbling brickwork, the grey blocks of flats were in a similar state of neglect to Gristle Street. Almost every square inch was covered in graffiti. Not the colourful kind in big bubble writing but scrawled swear words, spray-painted tags, insults and threats. The walkways outside the flats were littered with old rusty bikes and rubbish. On the grassy communal area a gang of lads threw stones at a three-legged dog.

'Home sweet home,' said Archie as the car pulled in.

Weaver dived out and opened the door.

The gang of lads noticed the car and lost interest in the dog.

Holly thought Archie looked nervous, but he smiled and said, 'See you tomorrow, then?'

'Holly won't be seeing anyone,' replied her dad. 'She's grounded.'

'Grounded?' she exclaimed. 'How long for?'

'For the rest of the summer.'

'Oi, nice car,' shouted one of the boys on the grass. 'Can I have a drive?'

Archie stepped out.

'Hey, that's little smelly-grove,' he yelled.

The others joined in.

'Yeah, I see your old man's nicked a new car?'

'Nah, his dad's still behind bars, eh, smell-growth?'

'I'll see you later, then,' said Archie, suddenly dashing across the lawn towards the block of flats on the far side.

The gang of boys took chase. Archie was quick and he beat them to the building, through the outer door and to the central staircase that led up to the flats. The gang followed him up the stairs, closing in.

Weaver slammed the car door and jumped into the

driver's seat. As they drove away, Holly twisted round to look out of the back window. Archie ran along the top walkway to a green door. She could feel his panic as he pounded on the door until it opened. He dived inside and the door shut, leaving the gang of boys outside. She didn't like to think what would have happened if they had caught him. Archie's heart must have been beating fast, but watching the scene from the car, with the gentle classical music playing, Holly felt distanced, like she was watching it on TV.

'Sit down properly,' snapped her dad irritably.

Holly did as she was told and neither of them spoke for the rest of the journey.

Outside her house, Weaver opened the door and Holly climbed out. Her dad led her back to the house. She glanced round to see Weaver disappear into the car and drive away.

'Go to your room,' said her dad.

Holly walked up the stairs miserably, her dad behind her. This wasn't the first time he had been upset with her. Every time she had been suspended or expelled from school, he had been upset with her. But this felt worse. This time she had embarrassed him at work. She opened her bedroom door and went in.

'There'll be no television, no computer and no

leaving the house. You'll stay in your room and think about what you've done. You're out of control,' said her dad, unplugging her computer and wheeling it out. He stopped in the doorway. 'You know, it's not just me. You've let your mother down too,' he said.

'That woman's not my mother!' exclaimed Holly.

Her dad looked at her sadly and said, 'I wasn't talking about Bridget. Your mother would never have approved of this kind of behaviour.'

He closed the door behind him.

Holly sat down on her bed and stared at the door. Tears built up in her eyes. She tried to hold them back but she couldn't help herself. She wasn't crying because her dad had shouted or because she was grounded or because she had lost Mrs Klingerflim's book. She cried because it was the first time her dad had spoken to her about Mum since the funeral.

Willow climbed out from under the bed and jumped into Holly's lap, letting out soft comforting miaows.

Chapter Eighteen

On a list of all the places in the world a Mountain Dragon is safe, a densely populated capital human city in the south-east of Britain wouldn't rate highly, and yet *safe* was exactly how Dirk always felt in London. It was his home, his patch. These rooftops were his playground.

'I still do not understand why we are coming back to this noisy humano nest?' said Alba.

'You don't need to understand,' said Dirk, landing on an old-fashioned red-brick library at a busy cross-roads. 'You need to keep quiet and stay close.'

He stood on his hind legs and worked out the best route. The lights changed and he leapt across the road, stopping on the roof of some flats above a row of shops. He looked back at Alba. She stared nervously down at a mother and two children coming out of the library, all clutching books to their chests.

'Come on,' mouthed Dirk.

Alba closed her eyes and made the jump, flying over the road, landing with a loud THUD on the roof.

'Frank, did you hear that? It sounded like something just landed on the roof,' shouted a woman's voice.

'It's probably those blasted squirrels,' another responded. 'I'll get the broom.'

Dirk grabbed Alba by the scruff of her neck, pressing his nose against hers.

'Will you be careful,' he whispered angrily. 'Keep your eyes open at all times. Use your wings to land gently. The roofs are your friends. Use them for cover. Now, come on.'

Dirk ran along the rooftops. He knew that Alba and London didn't mix well but he had no way of shaking her off and he needed to look at that book. He had no idea how, but the late Ivor Klingerflim had collected a lot of information and he hoped there was something in *Dragonlore* that would help him find a Sky Dragon and solve this case.

Dirk paused on a rooftop by a grassy roundabout near a row of shops. He looked down at the shoppers in the high street. Humans' love of shopping had always fascinated him. As far as Dirk could see shopping was a kind of hobby, and yet, looking down at the people trudging from store to store, they didn't appear to be enjoying themselves much. Big droplets of rain began to fall and the already disgruntled shoppers groaned and put up umbrellas.

The rain gave Dirk and Alba enough cover to move more quickly across the city. It wasn't long before they were soaring through Dirk's open office window.

Inside, Dirk pushed the window shut and picked up the remote control, out of habit pointing it at the TV, before remembering that Alba had smashed it.

'What does it do, this lights and noises box of yours?' asked Alba.

'It *was* a television,' replied Dirk pointedly. 'And before you broke it, it told me what was going on in the world,' he said, even though he spent much more time watching old detective films and reruns of cop shows than news programmes or serious documentaries.

Looking around the room he realised that Mrs Klingerflim had tidied up. There was no sign of the

book but on the desk was a note, written on the back
of the one he had left her. It read:

Mr Dilly,
I'm out until later tonight. I have tidied
up. Don't worry about the rent. Oh, and I
have lent dear Ivor's book to Holly. What
a lovely girl. So polite.
Yours,
Mrs K

'I've got to go out,' said Dirk, putting the note back
on the desk.

'I will be coming with you,' said Alba.

'Not this time. The city isn't safe for you. You can't
blend and you don't know these roofs like I do. You're
a quick dragon and you're in good shape, but for me
this is a full-time job.'

'But I must stay with you at all times.'

'Listen to me, Alba. We will find the Sky Dragon
and we will find your sister, but I can't risk you out
there again. Besides, I've got to go and visit a humano.
You wouldn't like that, would you?'

'Meet a humano? That would not be good.'

'OK, so stay here,' he replied. 'Keep the blinds down

and don't answer the door to anyone. If anyone knocks, I'm not in, you're not in, there's no one here, OK?'

'OK, I understand,' said Alba. She picked up a tin of beans. 'Can I eat some of your crunchy shelled food?'

'Knock yourself out, but you might want to try using this?' Dirk threw something at Alba.

'What is it?' asked Alba.

'It's called a tin opener,' he replied, moving the blinds out of his way and leaping out.

Across the road from Holly lived a nosy old woman called Mrs Baxter who spent her days sitting by her window, behind her net curtains, watching every single event in Elliot Drive and noting them down in her diary. If Mr Perry at forty-seven got an extra pint of milk delivered, or if Mrs Standen at forty-one had a longer than usual conversation with the postman, it went down in Mrs Baxter's diary.

She had noted that Holly Bigsby at forty-three hadn't left the house at all since she and her father had been spotted stepping out of a very expensive-looking silver car on Saturday. A blond-haired boy about her age had visited every day but had been sent away.

However, like all suburban gossips, Mrs Baxter

assumed that the most interesting events involved humans and therefore occurred at street level. Had she looked up at the roof, she would have seen a dragon squeeze through Holly's window. Instead, she was busy jotting down how Mr Mynard at number thirty-eight had left his car headlights on and would probably find in the morning that his battery had gone flat.

'Where have you been?' asked Holly, throwing her arms around Dirk's soft green belly. 'I kept trying to call.'

'I've been out of town on a case. That's why I'm here.'

'So you didn't come to see me,' said Holly, unable to hide her disappointment.

Dirk lifted her chin with his paw. 'I'm sorry, kiddo, I've been wrapped up in this case,' he said.

'What's it about?' she replied.

'Well, the newspaper headline would be "Sky Dragon kidnaps Sea Dragon",' said Dirk.

'Cool,' said Holly. 'What are Sky Dragons like?'

Dirk told Holly what little he knew about Sky Dragons and then said, 'The problem is they've been living in the clouds for a long time. No one knows much about them. I was hoping I'd be able to find something that might help in Mrs K's book.'

Holly looked away. 'Oh,' she said.

'*Oh* doesn't sound good,' said Dirk, picking up Willow, who had been rubbing herself against his leg, and stroking the cat.

'I haven't got it,' Holly admitted. 'It was confiscated.'

'Do you know where it is?'

'Well . . . Yes.'

'Fine. I'll swing by and grab it,' said Dirk.

'It won't be that easy,' said Holly.

'Come on.' Dirk spread his paws and grinned. 'Remember who you're talking to here.'

'It's been confiscated by the seventh richest man in the world, and is being kept in the upstairs office of a high-security animal experimentation lab,' said Holly.

Dirk laughed. He put Willow down. 'So you've been busy, then?' he said.

Holly told Dirk everything that had happened over the last two days. She told him about Brant Buchanan, her dad accepting a job for Global Sands, and the conversation she had overheard about the AOG Project.

'He must be after the QC3000,' said Dirk.

'That's what I thought but why would a billionaire businessman want a weapon?'

'I can think of lots of reasons,' he replied. 'For a man

135

like that, business *is* war. So how did he end up with the book?'

'I wanted to find out what they were up to, so I broke in, but I got caught.'

'They didn't see you blending, did they?'

'No, but I got taken upstairs and they took away the book as a punishment.'

'You think he knows what the book is?' asked Dirk, nervous about a human with so much wealth and power possessing a book that told the truth about dragonkind.

'I don't think so. He just thinks it's a stupid book for kids.'

'Tell me about the security.'

Holly recounted everything Mr Buchanan had told her about the building and how she had got in with Archie's help.

Dirk thought for a moment. 'We'll need a distraction,' he said.

'Archie could help again,' suggested Holly.

'No, the security guard might recognise him. Besides, I don't want any more humans knowing about me. We need someone he won't recognise, someone we can trust,' said Dirk, looking at her with a knowing wink.

'I'll make the call,' replied Holly, understanding instantly what that wink meant. 'What time?'

Dirk looked up at Holly's wall clock. He scratched his head uncertainly.

'Here, try this,' said Holly, showing him her watch.

He read the time: 19:01.

'Hey, digital,' said Dirk, smiling. 'How far's the lab?'

'It's about half an hour on the bus.'

'Tell him we need the distraction at a quarter to eight.'

Holly nodded and stepped out to make a phone call. As he waited, Dirk checked out her room. He had never been in it before. Everything was brightly coloured and all very Holly. On her desk were bits of paper with pencil-drawn pictures. He picked one up and recognised it as himself. He pulled open a drawer and saw the Shade-Hugger claw that they had discovered on their last case together. Dirk had forgotten all about it. She must have held on to it. It was against Dragonlore to let a human have any evidence of dragon existence, but if anyone could be trusted with it, it was Holly.

When she came back in, he said, 'I'm sorry I never returned your call.'

'That's OK,' she said. 'You're here now.'

'Won't your parents come and check on you?'

'No. My dad's out and his wife has a friend coming round, so she'll spend all evening drinking wine and smoking cigarettes in the garden.'

'Let's go, then.'

Across the road, Mrs Baxter was watching Mr Winter from number forty-five, who was having a very intimate conversation with a young blonde woman in a short skirt who certainly wasn't his wife. Taking down a full description of the woman, Mrs Baxter completely failed to notice the dragon slipping out of Holly Bigsby's bedroom window, dropping his tail down, hoisting the girl on to his back and disappearing across the rooftops.

Chapter Nineteen

With Holly's arms clung tightly around his neck, Dirk scampered across the row of residential roofs, expertly negotiating every aerial or satellite dish in his way, stepping on chimneys to gain extra height, flying from street to street, over gardens and backyards, before coming to a halt on a rooftop by the high street.

'There's a bus coming,' said Holly.

'Quick, blend with me,' ordered Dirk, turning roof-coloured.

Holly focused on what it would feel like to be Dirk's back blended with the roof tiles and vanished from sight just as the bus stopped next to them. She saw that its top deck was level with the roof where they were hiding.

The bus indicated right and pulled out.

'That's the problem with buses,' said Dirk. 'The top decks are ideal places for dragon-spotting.'

'So how do we avoid being seen?' asked Holly.

'We do what everyone else does,' he replied. 'We catch it. Hold tight.'

Dirk leapt off the roof, spread his wings and landed gently on top of the moving bus, gripping tightly with his claws.

Through the upstairs window of his house over-looking the high street, an overweight advertising executive was trying out the new running machine his wife had bought him, when he noticed a dragon with a girl on its back landing on top of a passing bus. He stopped the running machine, rubbed his eyes and looked again to find the bus still there but the dragon and the girl gone. Deciding that exercise clearly didn't agree with him, he went downstairs to the kitchen, where he found a large tub of strawberry-cheesecake-flavoured ice cream and a big spoon.

When the bus stopped outside the Global Sands laboratory, Dirk flew over the silver gates and landed on the flat roof of the lab. He poked his head over the edge and looked through the window at the office.

'It's empty,' he said.

Holly checked her watch. 'It's almost time,' she said.

Dirk got into position and pulled out a black sphere about the size of a golf ball from behind his right wing.

'Hold this,' he said, handing it to Holly.

'What is it?' she asked, inspecting it.

'It's a retroreflective camera–neutraliser. It sends invisible infrared lasers to block the security cameras.'

'Where did you get it?'

'I found it,' he replied, flicking out the claws on his right paw, checking the sharpness of each on his teeth, then plunging them into the roof. With the claws on his left paw he began to cut a hole.

'Mr Buchanan said nothing could cut through this roof,' said Holly.

'Buchanan has obviously never come across a dragon claw,' said Dirk.

Once he had made the hole, he pulled the piece of roof away. The polystyrene ceiling of Brant Buchanan's office was divided into square metres. Carefully he lifted one away, revealing the room below.

'What time are we on?' he asked, taking the black sphere off Holly.

'Thirty seconds,' replied Holly. 'I'll see if he's there.'

She crawled to the edge and looked over. In the alleyway, a man in a baseball cap was standing in front of the back door to the lab. The man checked his watch and swizzled his baseball cap around, revealing the well-worn face of Ladbroke Blake, the private detective who had once been hired to follow Holly and, ever since, helped her out whenever she most needed him. The baseball cap replaced his usual wide-brimmed hat. In place of his trench coat was a lurid red puffa jacket and in his hands was a large pizza box. He glanced at his watch, chucked a piece of gum into his mouth and pressed the intercom buzzer at precisely 19:45.

'Aye?' Hamish's voice came through the Intercom.

'Free pizza,' said Ladbroke, chewing the gum, speaking in a strong cockney accent.

'Ah didn't order a pizza.'

'Nah, mate, it's part of a promotional campaign. It's free, ain't it.'

'Ah can't go opening this door for a free pizza. Ah've got my job to think about here, laddie,' said Hamish.

'Fair enough, mate. I'll see if anyone else wants this free haggis pizza, then.'

142

'Did you say haggis pizza?' said Hamish, suddenly sounding interested.

'Yeah, it's one of our specials, sounds disgusting if you ask me.'

'Ah've never had a haggis pizza.'

'Whatever,' said Ladbroke.

'Well, Ah am a wee bit peckish. Stay there, Ah'm coming now.'

Ladbroke glanced around him. On the phone Holly hadn't told him where she would be or why she needed him to act as a distraction, and he hadn't asked. Holly always got the feeling that Ladbroke Blake had seen a lot more of the world than most people.

She nodded at Dirk and he dropped the camera-neutraliser into the room, waited for a second of two, then jumped in after it.

Dirk landed in a crouching position and quickly took in the layout of the office. Behind him was the glass desk. In front was the purple sofa. There was a door to his right, and on the ceiling were three cameras. He hoped the camera–neutraliser was working, otherwise the security guard was in for the shock of his life when he looked at the monitors only to find a dragon creeping around the room.

Holly's head appeared at the hole in the roof.

Dirk straightened up and grabbed her, lowering her down into the room.

'We need to be quick,' he said. 'Where's the book?'

'In the desk,' replied Holly, pointing to the glass desk, where the book was clearly visible in the drawer. She rounded it and tried to open it. 'It's locked,' she said.

Dirk slid the polystyrene ceiling square back over the ceiling and said, 'Go and keep a lookout while I pick the lock.'

Holly made her way down the stairs. At the bottom she stopped. She could hear footsteps. She looked through a glass pane in the door and saw the lithe grey figure of Weaver striding down the corridor, heading her way. She dived back into the stairwell and he walked straight past. She crept back out into the corridor. Weaver had gone into the room full of animal cages that she'd seen on her last visit.

Holly found the window that looked into the room. The bright overhead lighting flickered on and she saw Weaver carrying a plastic container with air holes along the top. He placed the container on a counter and pulled out what appeared to be a remote control from his pocket. He pressed a button. The container opened automatically and six white mice filed out, each walking to its designated cage. They were wearing the same metallic collars she had seen on the tabby cat.

Holly was distracted by the door at the end of the corridor opening again. Brant Buchanan entered, carrying a silver case in his right hand. His mobile phone rang and he paused to retrieve it from his pocket with his spare hand, giving Holly enough time to get out of the corridor and back up the stairs without being seen.

Chapter Twenty

Dirk pushed the tip of his smallest claw into the keyhole and jiggled it about. Picking locks was a fiddly business. Eventually he heard the click of the drawer being unlocked, but, before he could grab the book, the door burst open and Holly entered.

'Hide,' she whispered. 'Buchanan's coming. There's no time to get out.'

She ran to the side of the couch. Dirk dived into the corner by the desk. They both blended with their surroundings as the door opened.

From his position on the floor, Dirk watched Brant Buchanan cross the room. He placed the silver case on the desk, pulled up a chair and sat down. Through the glass, Dirk could read three letters on the base of the silver case; A, O and G.

'Hello, this is Hamish Fraser on security.' The voice came through the intercom.

'Yes, Hamish,' replied Buchanan.

'Is everything all right up there, Mr Buchanan, sir? The security cameras are out.'

'Everything's fine, thank you.'

'Right, then. Sorry to bother you.'

Buchanan pulled open the desk drawer and lifted out the red book with the white zigzag on the cover. He failed to notice that it should have been locked.

For a few moments they all sat in silence while Buchanan flicked through the book. The door opened and Dirk saw a man dressed in grey enter the room.

'Ah, Weaver, listen to this,' said Buchanan. '"Snow Dragons are one of the biggest challenges to a dragon-spotter",' he read aloud. '"Not only do they live in the furthermost regions of Antarctica but, being both white-bellied and white-backed, they are incredibly well camouflaged. If you are lucky and do get close enough to see one in detail you will notice that the underbelly is covered in a very fine fur. This provides excellent insulation against the cold."'

'Very interesting, sir,' said Weaver, sounding not at all interested.

'A white furry dragon, how sweet,' said Buchanan.

'Yes, sir.'

'Did you believe in dragons when you were a child, Weaver?' he asked.

'I can't remember, sir.'

'I did. It sounds stupid but I believed that the world was full of dragons. Only they were in hiding, waiting for the right time to attack us. The funny thing was, I wasn't scared. Do you know why?'

'No, sir,' said Weaver sounding like he didn't care either.

'Because for some reason I believed they would destroy everyone except for me.'

'We all think stupid things as children, sir,' said Weaver. 'Can we deal with the matter in hand now?'

'It's always work work work with you, Weaver,' sighed Buchanan, smiling.

'I'm sorry, sir. But don't you think this is more important than fairy stories about made-up creatures.'

'As usual, you are completely right,' admitted his boss. 'Show me how this thing works.'

Weaver reached over the desk, his grey shoes stepping dangerously close to Dirk's nose, and pressed buttons on either side of the silver case. It opened but Dirk couldn't see what it said on the screen.

'Normally it requires the Prime Minister's DNA authentication to operate,' Weaver said, 'but fortunately because of the recent government change we have acquired it during a handover period.'

'Meaning?'

'Anyone who knows how to use it can operate it.'

'And do we know how to use it?' Buchanan asked.

'Luckily, it came with instructions.' Weaver smiled and dropped a pamphlet on the desk.

Dirk read the cover:

AOG PROJECT
NAPOW TECHNOLOGY
THE VE 6.2 OPERATING MANUAL
TOP SECRET

'How very considerate of our friends in the Ministry of Defence,' said Buchanan.

'Ah'm sorry to bother you again, sir.' The security guard's voice came again from the intercom. 'You've got a visitor. Mr Malcolm Bigsby.'

'Thank you, send him up,' replied the billionaire.

'Are you sure this is wise? We barely know him,' said

Weaver, pacing anxiously.

'Relax. He's on the payroll. He's one of us now,' said Buchanan.

The door opened and Holly's dad entered.

'Ah, Malcolm,' said Buchanan in a welcoming tone. 'Look what we have here.'

Mr Bigsby looked at the silver case on the desk. 'But . . . but,' he stammered. 'But how did you steal it so quickly?'

'I don't like the word steal. The word I prefer is acquire, and I don't want you to get bogged down in the details of *how* we acquired it. The fact is we have what we want and it's all thanks to you.'

'You promised no one would get hurt?' said Mr Bigsby, sounding nervous.

'What do you take me for, a monster?'

'But the Ministry will be looking for it, won't they?'

Mr Buchanan laughed. 'Malcolm, you should know yourself that when something as top secret as this goes missing usual procedure is to deny that it exists at all. Looking for it draws too much attention.'

'Yes, that is true,' admitted Mr Bigsby.

Buchanan turned to Weaver. 'By the way, Weaver, good thinking knocking the security cameras out. You can't be too careful.'

'I haven't done anything to the cameras,' said Weaver, a sharp edge of anxiety in his voice.

'But Hamish said that they were . . .' Buchanan stopped mid-flow.

'You should get out of here,' said Weaver urgently. 'I'll do a proper sweep of the building, but you need to leave immediately.' Dirk could tell from his tone that this was an order not a request.

'You worry too much, Weaver. It's probably just a glitch. You know what technology is like, even our own.'

'All the same. Please, sir,' said Weaver firmly.

'All right. Come on, Malcolm, we'll give you a lift home?' said Buchanan, standing up. 'We can discuss your role at Global Sands on the way.'

'Thank you,' said Mr Bigsby.

Weaver picked up the silver case and hurried the two men out.

Two and a half minutes later, with his boss safe in the Bentley, Weaver returned to the office. Systematically he checked each camera. The red lights were on, which meant there was no fault with the equipment itself. He searched the room and discovered a small black sphere about the size of a golf ball. He picked it up and inspected it.

'Interesting,' he said to himself, dropping it into his pocket.

He walked to the desk and noticed that the instructions for the VE 6.2 and the red book with the white zigzag were no longer there.

'Very interesting,' he said, dropping to his knees and inspecting the floor. He found an area where the thick green carpet had been flattened. He jumped up with his arms outstretched and knocked the ceiling tile away. Where there should have been solid roof, there was a hole revealing the evening sky.

Weaver grabbed the chair from behind the desk, placed it below the hole and used it to climb out on to the roof. He scanned the rooftops and streets for any sign of the intruder, but whoever it was had gone. He looked closely at the jagged piece of roof that had been cut away.

'Extremely interesting,' he said, dropping back down into the office.

Chapter Twenty-One

Dirk stopped a couple of streets from his office on the flat roof of a Chinese takeaway, which had a good view of his window. The light was on and the blinds were pulled down.

'Aren't we going in?' asked Holly.

'No, Alba will freak out if she sees you. And don't you want to know what that silver case does first?'

Holly slipped off his back and opened the instructions for the VE 6.2, reading them out loud. '"The VE 6 dot 2 is the latest weapon to come from the AOG project. VE stands for Volcano Erupter. It uses the same sonar technology as the QC3000 to cause any targeted volcano in the world to suddenly erupt regardless of how dormant it is believed to be."'

'Another triumph for the AOG project,' said Dirk grimly.

'Why would anyone want a volcano to erupt?' asked Holly.

'Nature's weapons are the most powerful,' said Dirk. 'Volcanoes can wipe out entire cities; they can destabilise economies, not to mention the confusion and fear they create. And unlike conventional attacks, there's no one to retaliate against.'

'At least we have the instructions,' said Holly.

'True,' agreed Dirk. 'Now for Sky Dragons.'

He pulled out the copy of *Dragonlore* and turned to the chapter on Sky dragons, flicking quickly through the pages until he found what he was looking for. Holly put her arm around his neck and read it too.

In spite of keeping their distance from other dragons, Sky Dragons often travel in vast herds, communicating with each other using a type of telepathy beyond the reach of other dragons.

A keen dragon-spotter might find interesting the theory put forward by some experts that if another dragon were to spit liquid fire from the earth's Outer Core directly into the heart of a sublimated Sky Dragon it would be forced to materialise, similar to injecting a shot of adrenaline into a human heart to revive a man.

'I should take you home,' said Dirk.

'Can't I come in and meet Alba?' asked Holly.

'Sorry, Holly, this is dragon business. Besides, Alba's never come face to face with a human being.'

'Dirk, look!' exclaimed Holly, pointing to his office window, where the blinds were now up and there was a large shadow blocking the light. The shadow shifted and a Sea Dragon jumped out of the window, landing on the roof across the road, knocking off a satellite dish, sending it rolling down then smashing to the ground.

'Rats at a disco,' groaned Dirk. 'It's Alba. What's she up to?'

'I don't know,' replied Holly, 'but I think she may have come face to face with a human being now.'

On Alba's back, arms around her neck, was a blond boy. Holly recognised him at once.

'It's Archie,' she said.

'Your new friend?' replied Dirk, surprising himself with how jealous he sounded.

'Yeah, but how . . .' started Holly.

'I don't know,' interrupted Dirk, 'but they seem to be in a hurry. Come on.'

Following Alba, Dirk had to work extra hard to avoid being seen by all the Londoners trying to work out why their aerials and chimney tops had suddenly decided to fly off their roofs.

Alba eventually came to a standstill on the corrugated roof of a hut inside a yard full of beaten-up old cars. Dirk stopped on a nearby factory, keeping his distance. He looked around for an indication of where they were. On the side of a red-brick wall was a grubby street sign. Dirk read it.

'Now that is interesting,' he said.

'What is?' asked Holly.

'This street. It's Old Ford Street,' said Dirk.

'I've never heard of it,' said Holly.

'Neither had I until Alba asked me where it was. I thought she meant Oxford Street. Something's going on and I don't like it. Not one bit.'

Archie had knocked on Holly's door every day since Saturday, but every day her dad's big-haired wife had turned him away.

'She won't be seeing anybody,' she would say. 'You

156

should be ashamed of yourselves, dabbling in grown-up matters you don't understand.' Then she would slam the door in his face.

Archie didn't want to go back to his usual bunch of friends, hanging around the estate, complaining they were bored and trying to avoid being beaten up by the bigger kids. His day with Holly had been much more exciting.

After being told yet again by Big Hair to stop bothering her, Archie had gone to a sweetshop near Holly's house to restock on jelly beans. He stood outside, wondering what to do next. He opened the fresh packet, threw a jelly bean into his mouth and emptied the rest straight into his pockets, idly looking at the adverts on cards in the shop window. Amongst the usual ones for house cleaners, flats to rent and trombone lessons, one caught his eye. It read:

THE DRAGON DETECTIVE AGENCY
ALL CASES DEALT WITH
CONFIDENTIALLY AND WITH ALL DUE
DISCRETION

At the bottom of the advert was a phone number. Archie committed it to memory and ran to the nearest phone box. Having spent his only money on sweets he didn't have any change, so he called the freephone number for the telephone company.

He got through to a customer care agent, who introduced herself as Paula and asked how she could help.

Archie put on a deep voice and said, 'Yes, I'm phoning to report a fault on a line.'

'Certainly, sir. Is it the line you're calling from?'

'No, this is a phone box,' he said, reciting the telephone number for the Dragon Detective Agency.

Paula typed it into her computer and said, 'Can you confirm the address for that number?'

Archie held up the empty jelly-bean packet and scrunched it by the receiver as he pretended to give his address.

'I'm sorry,' said Paula. 'I didn't get that.'

Archie spoke a second time, again making it impossible to hear what he was saying with the sweet packet.

Paula asked once more but Archie did the same.

'I tell you what,' she said, getting frustrated, 'I'll read your address out and you tell me if that's right.'

'OK,' said Archie, smiling. He confirmed the address, put the phone down and jumped on a bus, which took him to the same house he had watched Holly enter a few days previously. He rang the bell and the white-haired old lady answered it.

'Hi, my name's Archie. I'm a friend of Holly's,' he said. 'I've come to see Mr Dilly.'

'I had a budgie called Archie once,' said the old lady irrelevantly. 'Is it short for anything?'

'Er . . . no,' replied Archie, thrown by this.

'My Ivor used to tell people his name was short for Ivordoodledandy. At parties after he'd had a bit too much to drink he used to swear blind that that was his name and just as he got someone to believe him, he'd admit he was joking. He was a silly man,' she chuckled.

'Is Mr Dilly in?' asked Archie, unsure how to respond to this story.

'I don't think he is,' she said.

Upstairs a loud CRASH rocked the whole building.

'Although I could be wrong,' she added, with a little wink. 'Let's go and see. Holly's told you about Mr Dilly, has she?'

'Oh yes, we're best friends; we don't have any secrets,' Archie said, following her upstairs.

'Mr Dilly,' she called, knocking on the door. 'Are you in, Mr Dilly?'

There was a pause then a female voice with a heavy foreign accent said, 'I am not in, Mr Dilly is not in, there is no one here.'

Chapter Twenty-Two

Alba recoiled in fear as the handle turned and she watched the door open. She tried to hide under the desk but, in her hurry, missed and whacked her head against the corner.

'Ouch!' She rubbed her head and found herself staring at two humans; an elderly female and a young male. The elderly female was smiling but the young male was staring, utterly gobsmacked.

'A ... a dragon,' stammered Archie, 'a real live dragon.'

'Actually, to be precise, she's a grey-backed, blue-bellied Sea Dragon,' said Mrs Klingerflim. 'Aren't you, dear?'

'You are humanos, I am breaching the forbidden

divide,' wailed Alba, trying to hide behind a newspaper but accidentally tearing it in two.

'Ivor and I used to spot Sea Dragons off the coast of Wales,' said Mrs Klingerflim fondly. 'You're Spanish, though, are you?'

'You knew there was a dragon in your house?' said Archie, looking at the old lady with as much astonishment as he had looked at Alba.

'Oh yes, but I didn't know there was a Sea Dragon,' she said, approaching Alba to inspect her more closely. 'Do you mind if I feel your back?'

'Stay away from me,' said Alba, edging backwards.

Mrs Klingerflim stroked Alba's tail and said, 'I'd say you've been out of the sea for a week or so. Am I right?'

'How is a humano knowing so much about our kind,' said Alba accusingly.

'My dear Ivor used to love Sea Dragons,' she replied. 'Sky Dragons have always been my favourite.'

'You know about Sky Dragons?'

'Oh yes, Ivor hated not being able to see them properly but that just made them more interesting to me. In fact I ended up writing the chapter on them.'

'Do you know how I could be finding one?' asked Alba.

'Well, you could always try summoning it?' said Mrs Klingerflim.

'How can I be doing this?'

'As I recall, you have to spit liquid fire from the Outer Core into a sublimated Sky Dragon's heart. Sounds like a terrible to-do, to me.'

Alba tilted her head to one side, digesting what she was being told. 'This really works?' she said.

'To be honest, I don't know for sure. Ivor used to tease me, saying it was just an old dragon's tale, but I believe it,' said Mrs Klingerflim. 'I've never had the chance to test it. You can't exactly buy liquid fire over the counter from Tesco's.'

'I do not know what is Tesco's but I must be going now,' Alba said, pulling up the blinds in front of the window. 'Do you know which direction I could find a humano place called Old Ford Street?'

'Old Ford Street? I'm afraid I don't know it,' said Mrs Klingerflim.

'Old Ford Street in Deptford?' said Archie, finally recovering from the shock of seeing a dragon. 'I know where it is; my dad used to have a business down there.'

'Where can I be finding number one hundred and seventy-six Old Ford Street?' asked Alba.

'I could show you,' he said. 'I could ride on your back.'

'It would be very bad to carry a humano,' said Alba nervously.

'Good luck finding it, then,' smiled Archie.

Alba thought for a moment before speaking. 'This is more important to me than the forbidden divide so I am deciding to let you show me the way.'

'Cool,' said Archie, climbing on to the desk and jumping on to the dragon's back.

'Ouch, you are kicking me.'

'Sorry. My name's Archie, by the way. What's yours?'

'Hello, Mr Archie. I am called Alba Longs,' replied Alba.

'What fun,' said Mrs Klingerflim, with a wistful glint in her eye. 'If I was twenty years younger I'd be coming along. You be careful.'

Alba opened the window and leapt out.

'This is so cool,' said Archie. He had never seen the city from this angle before. The sun was setting, turning the cloudy sky pink at the edge.

'Which way is the way?' said Alba, landing on a TV aerial, crushing it flat.

'Be careful,' said Archie as her tail sent a satellite dish flying. 'Head for that pub at the end of the street but mind the . . .'

His words were cut short by Alba knocking over a row of chimney tops like they were skittles.

As they made their way across the rooftops of London, leaving a trail of destruction in their wake, neither of them noticed that they were being followed.

They had been travelling for around half an hour when Archie said, 'We should be able to see the road from that block of flats.'

Alba made the jump, flying over a moving train that whizzed along a raised track, landing on the top of a building.

'Where is Old Ford Street?'

'That one,' said Archie, indicating a long dimly lit road, lined with dirty red-brick factory buildings, rubbish tips and breaker's yards, where old cars were smashed up and sold for spare parts.

Alba flew down to a factory roof.

Archie knew the area because his dad had once started a business further down the street. Archie had gone there a couple of times with him. He had enjoyed playing around the old cars until the business had gone the same way as all his old man's businesses and his dad had wound up in prison.

'There's one seven six,' said Archie, spotting the number written in red paint on the high gates of a down-beat breaker's yard.

Alba jumped from the top of a factory to a corrugated roof of a small shack inside the yard. Battered cars, with flaky paintwork and no wheels, were stacked up. There were piles of engines, exhausts, tyres and other car parts strewn around the place. In one corner was an upside-down yellow Mini. By the gates was an old reddish-coloured truck with its back doors hanging open, and, in the middle of the yard, was the empty shell of a once-white van.

'You must get off here,' said Alba.

Archie climbed off her back and pulled out a jelly bean from his pocket. 'Here,' he said, offering it to her.

'What is this small coloured pebble?' she asked cautiously.

'A jelly bean,' replied Archie. 'It's food.'

'Food? I am starving,' said Alba, taking it from his hand and throwing it into her throat. She swallowed it. Her eyes widened with delight. 'This is delicious. I very like this jelly bean. I very like it a lot. Have you more?'

Archie rummaged in his pocket and pulled out another and handed it to her.

'I do not know how to be thanking you for these jelly beans,' she said, 'but I must go and help for my sister.'

'Good luck,' said Archie.

'Thank you, Mr Archie,' she said, jumping down into the yard and prowling around, peering into gutted cars, looking for something.

A male voice called out, 'In here.'

Alba looked around, confused.

'I think it came from the truck,' said Archie.

Alba looked at the reddish-coloured truck. The back doors were open. 'Thank you, little humano,' she whispered, walking cautiously up the ramp into the back.

'Hello?' she called. 'Who is in there?'

The back doors of the truck suddenly swung shut and the engine started. Archie tried to see who was in the driver's seat but the angle was no good. The truck reversed, backing into the gates, pushing them wide open, swinging into the road.

Archie felt the corrugated iron roof buckle under the weight of something landing on it with such force that it knocked him off his feet. He looked up to see another dragon. This one had a green underbelly and a red back, and ears rather than gills. It peered at him with yellow eyes and spoke.

'So this is your friend, is it, Holly?'

Holly's head appeared over the dragon's shoulder. 'Dirk Dilly meet Archie Snellgrove,' she said.

Archie lowered his voice. 'There's another dragon,' he said.

'I know, it's Dirk,' said Holly, sliding off Dirk's back.

'There's another dragon,' repeated Archie.

'No kidding,' said Dirk. 'Where did Alba go? We lost sight of her. What was that truck doing?'

'There's *another* dragon,' he said for a third time.

'I think your friend might be a bit slow,' said Dirk.

'No,' insisted Archie, speaking through his teeth. 'Another one. Down there.'

Dirk craned his neck round to see a brown-backed, caramel-bellied Shade-Hugger stepping out of the shell of the once-white van, covering his eyes from the last rays of daylight.

'Karny,' muttered Dirk.

'Do you know this one too?' asked Archie.

'He's an old friend,' said Holly.

Chapter Twenty-Three

'Stay here, and keep quiet,' whispered Dirk, flying down to the yard, landing on Karnataka's back, catching the Shade-Hugger by surprise, pinning him to the ground.

'Cool uncle,' said Archie, grinning.

'You can't tell anyone,' said Holly.

'Who would believe me?' he replied, watching the two dragons struggling with each other.

'How's it going, Karny?' said Dirk in Karnataka's ear.

'Dirk Dilly,' he responded, in his usual nasal whine. 'I order you to release me.'

'Order me? You're getting ideas above your station,'

replied Dirk. 'All this power has gone to your . . .'

His words were cut short as a metal cuff slammed shut around his neck and his head was smashed into the side of a rusty Ford Capri.

'I think you'll find my station exactly matches my ideas, these days,' said Karnataka, 'seeing as I'm Captain of Dragnet now.' He stood up and brushed himself down. 'Good work, Officer Grunling.' He turned to Dirk and said, 'Balti here is my most trusted officer.'

Dirk pulled his head out of the dent it had made in the car door to see the dirt-brown Drake, whom he recognised as Dragnet Officer Balti Grunling.

'Oh, it's you,' said Balti to Dirk. 'You owe me pepper.'

Dirk had bribed Balti the last time they met with the promise of some pepper to liven up his otherwise rather plain mud diet.

'I'll get you all the pepper you need,' Dirk said.

Balti dragged his head into the car again, denting the dent, then he puffed out his chest and said, 'Assaulting Captain Karnataka the Fearless is an extremely serious offence. Shall I read him his rights, sir?'

'Not just yet,' said Karnataka. 'I need to speak to him in private. Leave us. I'll call when I need you.'

'I'm sorry, sir,' said Balti pompously, 'but that would be most irregular. This criminal attacked you.'

'As your captain, I order you to give me that chain and leave. Me and this dragon have business,' said Karnataka.

'Well, it's very unorthodox,' grumbled Officer Grunling, begrudgingly unhooking the chain from his tail, handing it to his superior, and walking into the shell of the once-white van. He muttered something in Dragonspeak that caused the rock beneath his feet to lower him into the ground.

Karnataka yanked hard on the chain, sending Dirk flying into the upside-down Mini, causing it to spin around on its roof and whack the back of his head.

Crouching on the corrugated iron roof, Archie whispered, 'I thought he said they were friends.'

'We need to help him,' said Holly.

'It's too high to jump down,' said Archie.

Holly slid to the back of the roof. 'Down here,' she said, disappearing over the edge.

Archie crawled to where she had been and looked down to see that Holly had landed on a large pile of tyres at the back of the building.

'Come on,' she mouthed.

On the other side of the shack Karnataka pounced

on Dirk, pulling the chain, yanking his head back.

'Spill the beans, Dirk,' he said in his nasal whine. 'You've found out, haven't you?'

'What beans? Found out what?' said Dirk, struggling to breathe.

'You must have found out how to contact a Sky Dragon by now.'

Karnataka had dragged Dirk's head so far back that Dirk was looking at him upside down. The angle was incredibly painful and not the most attractive view of Karnataka. Dirk could see right up his nose. So it was with great relief that Dirk watched a heavy lump of metal smash into Karnataka's head.

'Ow,' exclaimed the Shade-Hugger, loosening his grip on the chain.

A second piece of car engine collided with his head. Dirk took the opportunity to twist round and send a burst of fire into Karnataka's face. Karnataka screamed in pain and Dirk jumped up, reversing the situation, landing on top of him. He glanced up to see Holly and Archie standing nearby, poised with more bits of car at the ready.

'Thanks,' said Dirk.

'No problem,' replied Holly.

Dirk reached behind Karnataka's wing, retrieved a

key and undid the neck cuff, while holding Karny down with his other three sets of claws.

'Let me go,' said Karnataka.

'First things first,' replied Dirk. 'Something here doesn't add up. I found the line of ash after Alba had been to see you.'

'So what?'

'So how do you know about the Sky Dragons?'

'How? I . . . I . . . I'll tell you how. It's my job to know these things, that's h . . . how,' stammered Karnataka nervously.

'But if you knew about the Sky Dragons, that means . . .' Dirk stopped mid-flow. Somewhere inside his head a cog clicked into place. 'You set the whole thing up, didn't you, Karny?'

'I don't know what you mean,' said Karnataka, trying to avoid his gaze.

'You sent Alba to find me and lead me to her sister's cave. The ash outline wasn't real, was it? The idea was to make me think her sister's disappearance had something to do with a Sky Dragon. Shute was right. No Sky Dragon has materialised in hundreds of years. You tricked me. I bet Alba doesn't even have a sister.'

Karnataka writhed, trying to get free, but Dirk held him firmly.

'Delfina is real enough,' said Karnatka, 'real and in prison, arrested by Officer Grunling on some trumped-up charge of spying for the Kinghorns. You know how overzealous these Drakes can be with their arrests? When Alba came to me to plead for her release I came up with the plan to get her to hire you. I knew that your first stop would be the last place her sister was seen and that you'd find the outline of ash I made in her cave and assume that a Sky Dragon was responsible for her disappearance. Then it was only a matter of time before you found out how to contact the Sky Dragons.'

'I'll kill her,' snarled Dirk.

'Don't be too hard on her. I told her that if she failed I would banish Delfina with the other Kinghorn traitors, so she was trying to save her sister . . . save her from the Inner Core.'

'Why Sky Dragons?' asked Dirk.

'The Kinghorns are rising, Dirk,' replied Karnataka. 'They're waiting for the right time to attack. If we don't stop them it will be war, dragons against humans. The Drakes are tough enough but they haven't got the brains or power to defeat Vainclaw's army. Besides, offer them a big enough bribe and they'll swap sides before you can say liquorice laces.

We need allies, Dirk. We need the Skies on our side. You've heard the stories; they have powers beyond any of us. Firewalls, Dirk.'

Angry smoke poured from Dirk's nostrils. 'Why involve me?'

'Because I knew you could find the answer but I also knew if I asked you directly, you wouldn't help me.'

'You were right about that,' said Dirk.

'Alba was supposed to meet me at this address as soon as she learnt how to contact a Sky Dragon in exchange for her sister's release. I just got word from Balti that she was here. Where is she, anyway?'

'She got in a truck and it drove away,' said Archie.

Karnataka looked at the blond-haired boy. 'Not more of your human pets, Dirk?'

'This one wasn't my fault,' he replied. He turned to Archie. 'You mean she was in that truck we saw leave?'

'Yes, someone called her in and it drove off.'

'Where's the truck going, Karny?'

'I don't know anything about a truck. She was supposed to meet me here in exchange for her sister's release.'

'But if the truck is nothing to do with you . . .' began Dirk, his words trying to keep up with his racing thoughts. 'Who else knows about this place?'

'No one, just me and the Drake.'

Dirk swung his head to address Archie. 'What did the truck look like?' he asked.

'It was sort of reddish-coloured,' he replied.

'Anything else?'

'Only the two letters printed on the side.'

'What two letters?'

'G and S.'

'Global Sands,' gasped Holly.

'Rats on a stick,' exclaimed Dirk.

'You think Brant Buchanan knows more about dragons?' said Holly.

'I'm worried that it's looking that way,' said Dirk. 'Right, Captain Karnataka the Fearless, a Sea Dragon has been kidnapped by humans. It's time for you to live up to that name.'

'Ah, well . . . yes, right,' stumbled Karnataka, edging away. 'These days I have to follow correct Dragnet procedure. I'll alert the nearest duty officer, who will assemble an emergency action committee meeting.'

Dirk spat a mouthful of fire at him. 'If you don't help me I'll go before the Dragon Council and tell them what I know about those missing Welsh gold reserves.'

Karnataka could tell Dirk wasn't joking. 'All right,' he sighed. 'What do you want me to do?'

'Take the boy with you and search east. We'll look west.'

'You want me to carry a human? Are you mad?'

'While I'm chatting to the Council I could also mention this little Sky Dragon scheme of yours. I wonder how they'll view your actions,' added Dirk.

'But, Dirk . . . a human,' protested Karnataka.

'He'll help you identify the truck.'

Karnataka looked warily at Archie. 'All right, get on,' he said, 'but no kicking.'

Archie climbed on. 'Another dragon ride, brilliant!' he said happily.

'Whoever finds the truck first sends up a fire flare to let the other know where he is.'

'I'm the Captain of Dragnet,' whinged Karnataka. 'Do you know how risky carrying a human is for a dragon in my position?'

'You should have thought about that before you set me up,' said Dirk. 'Let's get going.'

Both dragons flew to the roof of the shack, Holly on Dirk's back, Archie on Karnataka's.

'And don't even think about ditching the kid and heading underground,' warned Dirk, 'It looks as though one of the most powerful humans on the planet has kidnapped a Sea Dragon. If we fail to rescue Alba you can kiss goodbye to your cushy job as captain and say hello to full-scale war.'

Chapter Twenty-Four

There were a surprisingly large number of reddish-coloured trucks in south-east London that evening. With the warmth of Holly's arms around his neck, Dirk searched the streets, but each time they found a truck that fitted the description, they would get close only to find it wasn't the one they were looking for. They had reached Waterloo, when Holly eventually spotted one with the letters G and S printed in white on the side.

'That's it,' she said.

Dirk soared over two parallel railway bridges and landed on the oval top of a cylindrical 3D cinema in the middle of a large traffic island.

'It's heading for the bridge,' he said.

The truck was crawling in traffic towards the river. Dirk jumped over an office block and landed on a rectangular pillar that jutted out of a building on the South Bank of the Thames. Holly recognised it as the National Theatre, having been there with Dad and Big Hair once to see a boring play about a man who spent four hours moaning about his dead father before getting into a fight and dying.

Below them, a crowd of theatre-goers had crammed themselves on to the balcony overlooking the river to enjoy an interval drink on this warm summer's evening. A bell rang twice, which Holly remembered meant two minutes until the second part of the play began.

Dirk took a deep breath and looked up at the sky, tilting his neck vertically. Holly struggled to cling on.

'What are you doing?' she asked, feeling his stomach swell.

He exhaled and Holly felt the skin around his neck get warm as a ball of fire flew from his mouth, shooting high into the London sky.

'It's a fire flare,' he said, 'so Karnataka will know which direction to head in.'

'Or which way to avoid,' said Holly cynically.

'Yes, he'll probably see it, dump Archie and head

back to Dragnet HQ,' agreed Dirk.

'The truck's getting away,' said Holly, seeing that it was already halfway across the bridge.

Dirk looked down. Jumping the river was always the most challenging part of his life in London. It meant a lot of open air, with no roofs to land on and blend into. It was OK late at night but in the low evening light with the babbling theatre crowd with nothing better to do than gaze across the river, it could be risky. Thankfully, the bell rang again, just once this time, and the balcony emptied.

'Hold tight,' said Dirk, taking half a step back then springing up, flying high over the river. Holly looked over Dirk's shoulder at the murky Thames water below, reflecting the darkening sky.

They landed on a quadrangular building on the north bank of the river, where they could see the truck following the road towards the centre of London.

Dirk ran across the building, vaulting over a line of statues that looked like they spent a lot of time in the company of pigeons. Across the rooftops he kept up with the truck as it drove through London's theatre-land, which bustled with energy and life.

'Why would they be taking a dragon further into

London?' asked Holly.

'There are lots of questions that need answering. How would Buchanan know where Alba was meeting Karnataka in the first place?' said Dirk.

The truck went up a one-way road, took a right then turned left towards an underground car park, but stopped suddenly as a black cab that had been trying to overtake on the inside slammed on its brakes and sounded its horn.

Holly looked up to see they were by an ugly skyscraper that towered above its neighbouring buildings. At the top its name was spelt out in capital letters. CENTRE POINT.

The truck driver waved a hand by way of apology and the taxi backed up, allowing the truck to turn.

'Get ready to blend,' said Dirk, jumping from a church to a grotty-looking pub, then to the top of the truck, where they vanished from sight.

'Oh no,' murmured Dirk. 'Height restriction.'

A yellow sign in the entrance stated the maximum height allowed into the car park. There was barely enough room for the truck, let alone the extra passengers on top. Holly rolled off Dirk's back and lay flat as the truck went in and the sign scraped across Dirk's back.

The truck drove down to the lowest level, where it came to a standstill. The car park had dim lights along the walls and concrete pillars that cast great dark shadows. On the far side was a service lift and stairs leading up. Except for the truck, the entire level was empty.

Holly heard the doors open and two people step out. Neither spoke as they slammed the doors shut and walked to the back of the truck, their footsteps echoing around the concrete walls.

The two men's features were shrouded in a dark shadow. They turned the door handles and stepped back, opening the doors, moving into the light so that Holly could see their faces.

'It's Arthur and Reg,' she gasped.

Arthur held a dusty, wooden-handled pistol, while Reg wielded a rusty old rifle. Holly remembered the war veteran across the road from Mrs Klingerflim. They must have stolen them from him. The weapons certainly looked like they belonged in a museum.

Something was stirring inside the truck. The long head of a dragon appeared beneath them, a thin line of smoke from its nostrils drifting up, making Holly's nose itch. She stifled the sneeze. The dragon stepped into the light.

'Alba,' Holly heard Dirk breathe.

'You must do what we say,' said Arthur, pointing the pistol at the Sea Dragon.

Alba glanced back into the van, then looked at Reg and said, 'I am not wanting any trouble.'

'No one need get hurt,' said Reg, waving his rifle at her.

'What's going on?' asked Holly softly into Dirk's ear.

Dirk motioned to stay quiet and they watched the two armed crooks escort the petrified Sea Dragon across the car park into the lift. The lift doors shut.

'I'm going after them,' said Dirk. 'You should stay here. This could prove dangerous.'

'I'm coming with you,' insisted Holly, climbing on to his back.

'There's no time to argue,' said Dirk.

'Exactly. Go,' she urged.

Dirk sprang from the roof of the truck and flew across the car park to the lift. He extended two claws, jammed them into the gap between the doors, and strained as he pulled them wide open to reveal the empty shaft. His whole body shook with the effort of holding them open. He pushed himself and Holly inside and they shut again. It was dark inside the shaft and filled with the sound of the lift rapidly ascending.

'Hold tight,' said Dirk. The shaft wasn't quite wide

enough to spread his wings and fly up, so he half-flew, half-scampered, using the ladder that ran up the side to propel himself faster. Holly held on as tightly as she could, locking her fingers together around his neck. They were gaining on the moving lift but she was being thrown about by Dirk, her legs flailing like a rag doll.

'Don't lose me,' she yelled desperately.

'I won't,' shouted Dirk above the squeaks of the lift. He tried to use his tail to secure her to his back, but lost his rhythm and collided with a wall just as Holly's left leg was outstretched. There was a CRUNCH and Holly yelped in pain.

'Hang on,' said Dirk, flapping one wing, giving him enough of a boost to grab on to the bottom of the lift, which was still hurtling upwards. He spun round, bringing himself face to face with Holly, so he was hanging upside down with her lying on his soft green underbelly.

'How are you doing, kiddo?' he asked.

Holly tried to smile but the pain she was feeling turned the smile into a grimace. The lift jolted violently as it reached the top of the shaft. Above them they heard footsteps as Alba Longs, Arthur Holt and Reginald Norman walked out.

Dirk jammed his claws into the underside of the lift, cutting straight through the base. He pulled his claw free and punched it until it bent back, making a hole big enough to climb through, then hauled them both inside.

Dirk placed Holly on the floor as gently as possible. Her jeans were stained with sticky red blood. Holly winced in pain as he examined her leg.

'I'm so sorry,' he said.

'Will it heal with sleep?' she asked, sucking her teeth.

'Not this time, Hol,' he replied. 'The bone's broken.'

Chapter Twenty-Five

'**W**here are we?' asked Holly.

'We must be at the top of Centre Point,' said Dirk. 'We need to get you to a hospital.'

'There's no time,' she replied. 'You've got to help Alba.'

Dirk knew she was right. Broken leg or no broken leg, two human crooks had a dragon held at gunpoint.

'Don't go anywhere,' he said.

'Like I've got any choice,' replied Holly, a spasm of pain crossing her face.

'Stay out of sight. I won't be long,' said Dirk, pressing the button to open the doors and stepping out, leaving Holly alone in the lift.

She looked at her leg. It was the same one that Vainclaw Grandin, the leader of the Kinghorns, had slashed in Little Hope. She wondered how she was going to explain a broken leg to her dad and his wife without admitting to leaving her room. Perhaps they had already discovered that she wasn't there and called the police.

She looked around for something to distract her from the pain. Above her was a row of buttons, each with the company name next to the relevant floor. She twisted herself around to get a better look, lifting herself on her hands, trying to avoid putting any weight on the broken leg. At the top she could see the white GS in block capitals on a red background, just like the one on the truck. Below it was the full company name in small writing. She strained to read it, but it was a difficult angle. She remembered how on the Global Sands website every division of the company used the same logo of a dark blue GS, with the curve of the letters forming a circle. It seemed strange that here in the lift and on the truck were the only times she had seen it written differently.

She pushed herself up the wall, bashing her leg and sending another shot of pain searing through her body. She tried again, this time raising herself high enough to read the tiny writing. She gasped. It didn't say Global Sands. The company name was Gronkong Shinard.

She had heard the name somewhere before. She couldn't quite place where. She felt the lift move and lost her footing, sliding down, knocking her leg. The pain was unbearable and she narrowly avoided slipping through the hole in the floor. She felt the lift judder. It was going down. She tried to reach a button to stop it, but she couldn't move her leg at all now.

Dirk stepped out of the lift on to the roof of Centre Point, high above the surrounding buildings of central London. The sounds of bus brakes, car stereos, taxi cabs, and hot-dog sellers drifted up from the streets. Alba Longs stood on her hind legs with her back to him. The two crooks were on either side of her, holding their guns in one hand and a large net in the other. Neither of them looked at Dirk.

'I am not sure I can do it,' said Alba.

'You must do what we say,' said Arthur.

'No one need get hurt,' added Reg.

'Are these two gentlemen bothering you, Alba?' asked Dirk casually.

The two men turned to look at him and Alba spun

around. She was holding the flask that Shute Hobcraft had given her.

'Mr Dirk,' she exclaimed. 'You have to go away. They will kill my sister.'

Arthur and Reg levelled their guns at Dirk's head.

'You must do what we say,' said Arthur.

'No one need get hurt,' said Reg.

'Change the record,' replied Dirk, springing into action, jumping up, twisting round, spinning horizontally through the air towards the unwitting crooks, using his tail to knock Arthur's gun out of his hands and grabbing Reg's rifle by the barrel, disarming both men. He yanked the net from their hands and threw it over their heads, bagging both of them. Dirk lifted the net to look at the two crooks, squashed together inside.

'You must do what we say,' said Arthur.

'No one need get hurt,' said Reg.

He recognised the look in their eyes instantly. It was the same look he had seen in the eyes of the Prime Minister in Little Hope Village Hall. It was the same look he had seen in his mother's eyes, when he had found her dead body many years ago. They were under the spell of Dragonsong. He felt a surge of fury.

'Oh, Mr Dirk. What have you done? Now they will

kill Delfina.'

'What are you talking about? Karnataka has Delfina locked up. I know you've been lying to me.'

'You are right,' said Alba, averting her eyes. 'I have been a liar to you but not now. Delfina is no longer in the prison.'

'Where is she, then?' demanded Dirk.

Behind him he heard the *ting!* of the lift door opening. He turned around to see smoke billowing out like it had caught on fire.

'Holly,' he said, putting the net down and jumping forward, but, before he got too close, he saw something shift inside the smoke. From within the lift emerged a Mountain Dragon, like Dirk, but larger, leaner and darker, and with grey smoke pouring uncontrollably from its nose. The Mountain Dragon's predatory eyes fell on Dirk and its mouth curled into a sinister smile.

'Vainclaw Grandin,' snarled Dirk.

'Dirk Dilly, the dragon detective,' replied the deep baritone voice.

'Whatever you're planning, it's over. I've got your henchmen bagged.'

'Henchmen, yes . . . Not my hench dragons, though,' replied Vainclaw.

Behind him from the lift emerged Leon, the eldest of the two yellow-backed Scavenger brothers who worked for Vainclaw. He was holding a Sea Dragon, a claw jammed threateningly into her jaw.

'Delfina,' said Alba desperately. 'Are you all right?'

'Don't let them hurt me, Alba,' whimpered her sister. She looked terrified.

'Keep quiet, hard-back,' growled Leon.

A second Scavenger climbed up through the hole Dirk had made in the lift and picked up what looked like a blood-stained bundle of clothes. As he stepped out on to the roof, Dirk could see that he was holding Holly, the blood from her leg smeared across his belly.

'Ar-right, Mr Detective,' he said. 'I've got your little friend here.'

'I'm sorry, Dirk,' she said.

'If you hurt her I'll roast your heart out, Scavenger,' replied Dirk.

'You want me to chuck her over so we can have a fair fight?' replied Mali, waving Holly over the edge of the building.

'Not yet, ar kid,' snapped his brother.

'You never let me have any fun, bro,' replied Mali.

'Cease your bickering,' said Vainclaw. 'We have work to do.'

Chapter Twenty-Six

'Now, Mr Dilly, we are thirty-five floors above a hard concrete pavement,' said the deep voice of Vainclaw Grandin, 'so you will do everything I say otherwise my Scavenger will let go of the girl.'

'Yeah, I'll give her a free flying lesson,' said Mali, leaning forward and forcing Holly to see how high up she was.

'There will be no tricks,' said Vainclaw. 'Is that clear?'

'As crystal,' said Dirk, through gritted teeth.

'I'm sorry, Dirk,' said Holly. 'I realised just after you'd gone. GS doesn't stand for Global Sands . . .'

'Eh, who rattled your cage?' said Mali, shaking Holly so that her bad leg flew about, causing her to cry out. Tears streamed down her face.

'GS stands for Gronkong Shinard.' Vainclaw finished her sentence.

Dirk knew the name. When he first discovered Kinghorns in London they had been hiding in a warehouse that was registered to a Gronkong Shinard.

'What is it?' he asked.

'Rearrange the letters to find our true identity.'

It only took Dirk a moment to come up with the answer. 'Kinghorn Dragons,' he muttered. 'But why would the Kinghorns have a company in the human world?'

'How naive you are,' said Vainclaw, pulling the net off Arthur and Reg and checking that they were still under the Dragonsong spell. 'Gronkong Shinard has been operating for a long, long time. Gronkong Shinard built this tower.'

'This is a modern building,' said Dirk. 'It was built by men.'

'The outside is modern, yes,' said Vainclaw, 'but the men constructed it around a central stone spine which dates back to a time when dragons used to help humans build their monuments in return for gold. The pyramids, Stonehenge, the Aztec temples, the Great Wall of China, all built with the help of gold-greedy dragons. But with this tower, Gronkong Shinard retained the rights to the top floor and roof. At the base of the foundations is an entrance that allows us to come and go as we please. So you see our headquarters are in the heart of the human civilisation that we will soon destroy.'

Arthur and Reg picked up the old weapons and turned them on Alba.

'You know what to do, Alba Longs,' said Vainclaw.

'Please, no. I have told you how to be summoning a Sky Dragon. Why can you not let me go now and summon one for yourself?'

'Because no Sky Dragon will trust the dragon who summons it,' replied Vainclaw. 'It will believe that my Kinghorns and I have come to its rescue.'

'You really think you can convince the Skies to join you with a cheap trick like that?' said Dirk.

'Please don't make me do it,' begged Alba.

Vainclaw smiled. 'It's your lucky day, Alba Longs, it seems we have another candidate. Humans, aim your weapons at this dragon,' he urged, pointing at Dirk.

The two crooks altered their aim accordingly.

'As luck would have it a herd of Sky Dragons is passing over London at this moment,' continued Vainclaw. 'We only need one of them. I understand that the suggested method is to spit the liquid fire into the heart, Mr Dilly.'

Dirk glanced at Mali holding Holly over the edge of the building.

'Don't do it, Dirk,' she cried.

'You wouldn't want me to drop her, would you?' said the yellow-backed Scavenger, letting her slide a little.

'All right,' said Dirk. He took the flask from Alba and flipped the top open. Inside, the scorching liquid was sizzling and hissing like it was alive. The tiny sip he had taken at the Outer Core had been painful enough. In order to reach a Sky Dragon he would have to take a big gulp. It wasn't going to be fun.

'In your own time, detective,' said Vainclaw.

Dirk considered his options. If it hadn't been for Holly he could have used the liquid fire as a weapon, but he could tell that Mali was waiting for an excuse to drop her and he had no doubt that Vainclaw would happily give the order. He had no choice but to do as Vainclaw said.

He looked up at the overcast sky. Even though it was night, the light pollution in the city meant that the London sky never went fully dark. He stared up at the clouds, trying to distinguish a shape amongst them. It brought back a long-forgotten memory of being a very young dragon lying on a mountainside with his mother, looking up at the sky, trying to spot sublimated Sky Dragons.

'Hurry up,' growled Vainclaw.

'You must do what we say,' said Arthur.

'No one need get hurt,' said Reg.

A cloud drifted past, lower and faster moving than the others. Dirk raised his head, trying to make out a dragon shape. He thought he could see a head and two wings.

'Bottoms up,' he said, shutting his eyes in anticipation of the pain before taking a large swig from the flask, holding the liquid fire in the back of his throat and tipping his head back.

The pain tore through his body, scorching his insides. He screamed in agony and spat out the liquid fire. It shot up into the sky like a burning arrow but he had misjudged how quickly the dragon-shaped cloud was moving. It missed. The jet of liquid fire lingered for a moment in the sky before vanishing into nothing. Dirk collapsed to his knees.

'Try again,' said Vainclaw patiently.

'Water,' uttered Dirk, his throat feeling like a desert. He could have devoured an iceberg like it was a lollipop. The last thing he wanted to do was take another swig of the burning liquid, but he focused on Holly being held over the edge of the building. He thought he could hear her saying something but the sounds around him were blending into one.

'Hurry up, detective,' said Vainclaw's deep voice.

Dirk struggled back to his feet. He looked up again. Another low cloud was coming. Again he picked out the outline of a dragon. He lifted the flask to his lips and poured. The agony was excruciating. His vision was blurred but he steadied himself, took aim and spat the fire high into the sky.

This time the liquid got the cloud, but it was off target, not quite hitting where the heart would have been.

Dirk fell on to all fours, his head bowed. He felt like he had sunburnt his insides. He couldn't speak. His vision was blurred but he heard that distinctive baritone say, 'If you don't get one, the girl will be pavement jam.'

Dirk stood up with his last bit of energy and checked the flask. There was only enough left for one more attempt. He picked out another low cloud in the shape of a dragon. He took the final gulp of liquid fire and held it in his throat. It felt like it was going to burn a hole straight through his skin. He waited for the right moment, trying to focus, and then released it.

'Aghhhhyeahh,' he screamed as the orange liquid shot from his mouth, piercing the cloud.

This time it was on target. Instantly the cloud began to bubble and hiss angrily.

'Get ready,' said Vainclaw.

The cloud above came tumbling down, swirling like an out-of-control helicopter. The soft blurry edges took form, like a photograph being developed. A tail appeared, a body, wings, a long sleek neck and, finally, a head. The materialised Sky Dragon was about the same size as Dirk but with a longer head and tail and a much larger wingspan. Its back was sky blue, its belly, cloud-white. It landed on top of the building, clasped its paws to its heart in pain, tried to stay on its feet, but slumped on to its belly.

Dirk gasped for breath, feeling like his insides had been cooked. He could barely speak but he managed to mutter, 'I'm sorry,' before he passed out altogether.

Chapter Twenty-Seven

'**N**ooo,' cried Holly, watching Dirk collapse into a heap.

'Eh, little girl, keep a lid on it,' said Mali. Holly could feel his warm stinking breath on her face. She looked down. It was a long way to fall. Below, normal people in the streets went about their normal lives, doing normal things, as though it was just a normal Tuesday evening in the middle of London, unaware of the drama unfolding above them.

The Sky Dragon was blocking Holly's view of Dirk. It looked weak and tired. In the centre of its blue back was a black burn mark, where the liquid fire had torn through its body. It coughed, and a cloud of ash flew off its skin, like dust being beaten from a pillow, landing on the ground, producing an outline around its body. It raised its enormous head wearily and looked at her. She noticed that, unlike most dragon eyes, which were yellow, its eyes were creamy and reflective.

Arthur and Reg threw the net over the poor creature. It tried to free itself, but clearly didn't have the energy.

'What is your name, Sky Dragon?' said Vainclaw, bending low to speak in its ear.

'My name is Nebula Colorado,' it replied. It was a female and spoke with a voice as soft as a summer's breeze.

'It is humans who have done this to you,' said Vainclaw. 'Together with this Mountain Dragon they summoned you in order to kill you. We came to save your life. Stand back, humans.'

Arthur and Reg silently obeyed.

'It's a trick,' shouted Holly with all the energy she could muster. 'Don't listen to . . .'

Mali clasped a clammy paw over her mouth, preventing her from speaking.

'Send for help,' urged Vainclaw, his words dripping like poison. 'The humans are planning to attack. The Kinghorns need allies if we are to defeat them.

Mankind has awoken to the reality of dragons. It is time for action before all your brothers and sisters are summoned and slaughtered.'

The Sky Dragon opened its mouth again and spoke. 'I have called the Skies. They are coming,' she said, shutting her eyes.

Vainclaw inspected the body. 'She's unconscious,' he announced.

Where are you, Dirk? Holly thought hard, remembering how he had spoken in her head when they had been up against the Kinghorns the last time. There was no response.

Vainclaw turned to Holly, smoke pouring from his nose. 'I imagine you're waiting for your detective to save the day,' he said.

Holly didn't answer, trying not to look at how far from the ground she was.

'Alba Longs, check on Mr Dilly,' ordered Vainclaw. 'Do it quickly or Leon will slice up your sister.'

'They mean what they say,' said Delfina, her voice quivering with fear.

'That's right. I'll cut up your sister and feed her to the pigeons,' said Leon, digging his claw further into Delfina's chin.

Shaking with every step, Alba made her way around

the Sky Dragon. 'Mr Dirk is still here,' she said. 'There is no movements from him at all.'

'You see, little girl?' said Vainclaw to Holly. 'We've won. All we have to do now is wait for the other Sky Dragons to appear, then we will take our new allies straight down to the Outer Core to build up their strength ready for the beginning of the war. Dragons against humans. Who's your money on?'

'Eh, boss,' said Mali, sounding nervous. 'Won't the humans notice all them Skies appearing over the city?'

'Who cares?' snapped Vainclaw, with a dismissive wave. 'The time is upon us. We have waited too long for the right time. Finally, we will have the ultimate weapons . . . Sky Dragons. Let these upright mammals convince themselves on their idiotic TV shows that the sightings above London were just hallucinations brought on by some chemical in the water. With the Skies on our side, all of dragonkind will join us. Then we will pluck this over-ripe race from their position of power. Once we have won they will bow down to their new dragon masters. Kinghorns will rule them all, and I, Vainclaw Grandin, the first up-airer, will rule the world.' Vainclaw shouted these words triumphantly.

'Nice speech, boss,' said Leon.

'Yeah, it was really stirring and all,' nodded Mali enthusiastically.

'It won't work,' said Holly weakly.

Vainclaw looked at her with an amused smile. 'What would you know, a mere human child?'

'You won't be able to trick the Sky Dragons. They won't join you,' said Holly stubbornly. 'I could see it in her eyes. There was kindness. She won't help destroy us. None of them will.'

'Eh, boss, shall I drop her?' said Mali, holding her over the edge.

Vainclaw reached out a long claw and touched Holly's hair, blowing pungent smoke in her face, then turned his back and nodded.

'Yes, drop her,' he said.

Holly felt Mali's grip loosen.

He let go and she fell.

When Karnataka had seen the fire flare, his first instinct was to ignore it, but Archie, who had been enjoying his second dragon ride of the evening, saw it too and said, 'What's that?'

'It's nothing,' said Karny dismissively. 'Probably a shooting star.'

'No it's not. It's what he talked about; a fire flare,

isn't it?' he said, remembering Dirk's words back in the yard. 'That means they've found the van.'

In spite of the danger, Archie was having the best night of his life. He had already met three dragons and now it was up to him to persuade this one to do the right thing.

'OK, so maybe it does,' admitted Karnataka. 'So we can go home. I'll drop you off at the nearest station.'

'We should go and help them,' said Archie. He had noticed Karnataka hadn't exactly been searching very hard for the van.

'Why?' snapped Karny.

'Because from what I heard back there this is all your fault,' replied Archie resolutely.

They came to a rest on top of a bakery with air vents churning out delicious smells. Karnataka craned his head round to look at Archie. 'You don't know anything, human.'

'I know you're a coward who won't go and help someone who's supposed to be a friend,' said Archie.

'So what?' said Karnataka in his high-pitched whine, pacing around an air vent. 'So what if I'm a coward? What's so good about being brave, anyway? Cowards stay alive, particularly smart cowards.'

'I don't think you are smart,' said Archie pointedly.

'I don't care what a human kid thinks. I'm not going,' stated Karnataka.

'A dragon who was working for you has been kidnapped by humans.'

'So what?'

'So as far as I understand you're quite an important dragon.'

'A very important dragon,' interjected Karnataka.

'Isn't that going to bring up some difficult questions . . . questions you don't want to answer? Like, what was she doing for you and whether the whole thing is your fault?'

'Well, yes,' admitted Karnataka.

'So the truly cowardly thing to do would be to go help rescue her and avoid all that hassle.'

Karnataka breathed in the smell of fresh bread from the shop. 'Yes, I suppose you're right.'

'Brilliant. Let's go,' said Archie, beaming.

'You're pretty smart for a human,' Karnataka said bitterly. 'Don't tell anyone I admitted to being a coward. I have a reputation to maintain, you know.'

Karnataka jumped across the road to another roof, heading towards the Thames where the flare had come from.

After they crossed the river the trail went cold. No

more flares went up and they couldn't find any trace of the reddish-coloured van.

'Well, we've tried our best,' said Karnataka.

'What's that?' Archie was looking at an orange streak in the sky. 'It's coming from that tall building.'

Karnataka landed on a low roof near the tower, above a trendy bar which was playing loud electronic music. He could feel the vibration of the bass line beneath his feet. The clink of glasses and hum of human chatter rose up into the warm night air.

'We should go up,' Archie said.

'This is close enough,' replied Karnataka.

A second streak of light flashed above the tall building. Then a third. It looked as though something appeared in the sky then fell out of sight on to the roof. It was impossible to say what.

'What's happening?' asked Archie.

'I don't know,' said Karnataka.

They continued to watch. Something was being dangled over the edge of the building.

'What's that?' exclaimed Archie.

A girl's scream cut through the air.

'It's Holly, go!' shouted Archie, kicking his heels into Karnataka's belly, like he was geeing up a horse.

Shocked by the firmness of the voice and the

hardness of the kick, Karnataka obeyed unquestioningly. He spread his wings and flew to the building, where he positioned himself under the falling girl.

'Hold on,' he said. Archie gripped tightly as Karnataka swivelled upside down, causing him to dangle precariously from his neck. There was a jolt and Archie almost lost his grip as Holly landed on the Shade-Hugger's soft underbelly. Karnataka clamped a forearm over the girl, holding her safely in place, then turned vertically and flew upwards.

Chapter Twenty-Eight

Flying up the side of the building, Holly and Archie found themselves face to face over Karnataka's shoulder.

'Good timing,' said Holly weakly.

'What's wrong?' asked Archie, seeing she was in pain.

'My leg's broken and Dirk's passed out.'

'Who's up there?' asked Karnataka, slowing down.

'Leon and Mali are holding Alba's sister hostage. Vainclaw is making it look like Arthur and Reg have caught the Sky Dragon.'

'Vainclaw Grandin?' said Karnataka, changing direction, heading down.

'What are you doing?' said Holly and Archie together.

'Three Kinghorns against one me?' said Karnataka. 'Not my sort of odds.'

'If you don't do something the Sky Dragons will appear and then no one will be able to stop the war,' said Holly.

'Which would make your job very difficult,' added Archie. 'It's the cowardly thing to do. You know I'm right.'

'You're really starting to bug me,' said Karnataka, changing direction again and flying back up the side of the building towards the top, zooming past the floors of empty offices.

Above them, on the roof, Mali was looking down. 'It's the Shade-Hugger, the one that took your job, bro. He's rescued the girl and he's got another kid. Can I go and get him?'

'No,' said Vainclaw firmly. 'Let him land. From all I hear about this Captain Karnataka it will be easy enough to persuade him to switch sides.'

Karnataka landed on his hind legs next to Dirk's unconscious body. He placed Holly down beside Dirk and Archie jumped off.

'Dirk? Are you all right?' said Holly, draping an arm over his shoulder. Dirk made no response. Holly rested her head on his and closed her eyes.

'How gloriously pathetic,' said Vainclaw. 'Welcome, Captain Karnataka. Firstly, let me congratulate you on this marvellous Sky Dragon plan. How inventive you are.'

'Mr Captain Karnataka,' said Alba. 'You told me you had Delfina, but these Kinghorns have got her?'

'Keep quiet, Sea Dragon,' said Leon, 'else I'll cut your sister's throat.'

'I do not think he is fooling,' said Delfina, sounding terrified.

'Enough,' barked Vainclaw. 'Shade-Hugger, I'm going to come straight to the point. I have a proposal. Shortly, the rest of the Sky Dragons will appear. Look, they are already gathering.'

Karnataka looked to see that the edge of the purple sky was blackening as though a storm was approaching, closing in from every corner of the sky. The sublimated Sky Dragons were nearing.

'I'll give you one chance. Join us now and you can be one of us. The Kinghorns always have time for a dragon of your moral flexibility.'

Karnataka glanced back at Archie.

'You can't do it,' said Archie.

'Sorry,' shrugged Karnataka. 'I told you I was a coward.' He walked towards Vainclaw, edging around the Sky Dragon. 'You've got yourself a deal,' he said.

'I knew you were my kind of dragon,' said Vainclaw.

Archie leant over Holly and whispered in Dirk's ear, 'What can I do?'

For a moment there was nothing. Then a tiny puff of smoke drifted up from Dirk's nostrils.

'What can I do?' repeated Archie.

The smoke formed into shapes. They were weak and only lasted a second but Archie made out three letters: S K Y.

Archie looked up. The blackening edge of the sky was getting near, closing in on London. The three smoke letters blended together and formed into the shape of an arrow, which pointed to the large unconscious dragon in the centre of the roof.

'Kinghorns prepare,' said Vainclaw. 'When they arrive we'll kill the humans as though we are rescuing the Sky Dragon from them.'

Reg and Arthur remained oblivious to his words, helplessly awaiting their fate.

Archie snuck around the Sky Dragon's large body, crawling through the thick line of ash that surrounded it. He reached the head and pulled back the net.

'Hey,' he said in the Sky Dragon's ear. 'Hey, Sky Dragon, wake up.' Nothing. Archie tried to lift up one of its huge eyelids, but it was as though it was locked shut. Then the corner of the dragon's mouth moved and it spoke softly.

'Too weak,' she said. 'Need sugar.'

'Sugar?' said Archie.

The circle of sky drew in, as the black cloud army neared. Leon pushed Delfina away, and the two scavengers stood in front of Arthur and Reg, ready to kill them when Vainclaw gave the word.

'Delfina? Are you OK?' said Alba.

Before Alba's sister could respond, Karnataka leapt into the air, kicking Mali in the ear and whacking Leon with his tail, before landing on top of Vainclaw, pinning him down with his claws. 'Alba and Delfina, get the Scavengers,' he cried.

'Get off me,' snarled Vainclaw. 'What are you doing?'

'Making it better odds,' replied Karnataka. 'Now it's three all.'

'Actually it is four two.' He heard the voice in his ear and felt a claw around his throat. 'Get off the boss.'

'Delfina?' said Alba in surprise. 'What are you doing? Captain Karnataka is on our side.'

Delfina forced Karnataka off Vainclaw, with her sharp claws pressed against his neck. 'You're wrong, sister,' she said. 'I am on the same side as my leader, Vainclaw Grandin.'

'You . . . You are . . . You are a Kinghorn?' stammered Alba.

'I am a dragon, sister,' she replied, 'and proud to be a dragon. I was spying for Vainclaw when that stupid Drake arrested me.' She laughed. 'You see, sometimes they get it right.'

Delfina pushed a claw into Karnataka's ribs, piercing the skin, causing green blood to ooze out.

The circle of sky was the same circumference as the tower and the dark clouds were beginning to swoop down. In the streets below the humans ran for cover, fearing a storm. But no rain fell. Instead, the sky began to bubble and sizzle, as though it was on fire.

'What a shame, Captain Karnataka,' said Vainclaw Grandin. 'You're about to watch the dawn of a new era and you've just blown your chance of being a part of it.'

Then a voice spoke, drifting through the air like a gust of wind.

'It's too early for dawn,' it said.

Vainclaw spun around to see Nebula Colorado, the

Sky Dragon looming over him, standing tall on her hind legs, head raised to the sky.

'Another jelly bean?' said Archie.

'Thank you,' said Nebula.

Chapter Twenty-Nine

'Sky Dragon . . . Nebula . . . friend,' Vainclaw spoke slowly, emphasising each word. 'Your anger should be directed at these human aggressors.'

The Sky Dragon's milk-white eyes focused on Arthur and Reg, who swayed a little.

'Dragonsong has been used on these humans,' she said.

'The Skies must join the Kinghorns,' growled Vainclaw threateningly.

'I have already called my siblings off,' said Nebula.

Vainclaw Grandin, the Scavenger brothers, the Sea Dragon sisters, Karnataka and Archie all looked at the circle of sky, visible above the dark cloud of gathering

Sky Dragons.

It was widening.

The Sky Dragons were retreating.

Only Arthur, Reg, Dirk and Holly remained oblivious to this spectacular sight; the crooks still under the spell of Dragonsong, Dirk unconscious, Holly in too much pain to lift her head.

Vainclaw's eyes narrowed. 'If you won't join us step aside so we can rid ourselves of this incompetent captain and this interfering detective,' he said, lowering his head.

'You will harm no one,' said Nebula, spreading her wings to block his way.

'No one need get harmed,' said Reg automatically.

'You must do exactly as we say,' added Arthur.

'You idiotic humans with your pathetic toy guns,' snapped Vainclaw irritably. 'You are no longer needed. Take the lift and leave us.'

Without argument Arthur and Reg walked to the lift, pressed the button to go down and disappeared behind the sliding doors.

'I knew you'd pick the right side,' said Karnataka, standing behind Nebula's wing.

Nebula lowered her wings and turned to look at him. 'The Sky Dragons do not pick sides.'

'But he wants to start a war,' protested Karnataka petulantly.

'And you want to stop it,' she replied patiently. 'Yes, I do understand, but it is our policy not to take sides in earthly matters.'

'What about right and wrong?' insisted Karnataka.

'There is an old Sky Dragon saying,' said Nebula. 'Exist simply and simply exist.'

'We Kinghorns have a saying too,' growled Vainclaw darkly. 'Those who stand in our way will not stand for long.'

All four Kinghorns moved into attack formation, heads lowered, claws drawn, smoke gushing threateningly from their nostrils. Vainclaw and Leon stood to the right, Mali and Delfina on the left. Karnataka edged back, stepping on Dirk's tail, causing him to let out a low groan. Alba looked back and forth between the Kinghorns and the Sky Dragon, unsure what to do.

'It is time for you to pick a side as well, sister,' said Delfina. 'Join us or betray your kind.'

Alba looked into her sister's yellow eyes. 'It is you that is being the traitor,' she spat. 'You are no longer my sister.'

She moved next to Nebula. 'I, Alba Longs, will fight

you and help save Mr Dirk,' she said.

'Stand behind me,' said Nebula calmly.

'You are the boss, Miss Nebula,' said Alba, quickly moving back, standing on Dirk's paw, causing him to let out another moan. 'Very sorry, Mr Dirk,' she said.

'Let's see what this Sky Dragon has got, then?' jeered Leon.

'Yeah, give us your best shot,' goaded Mali.

Nebula opened her mouth and swung her head round, making an awful rasping noise, but nothing came out.

'She's got no fire,' cackled Mali.

'Perhaps the child's sweets weren't quite enough to fully restore you,' said Vainclaw.

Holly stirred. 'What's going on?' she asked weakly, opening her eyes for a moment.

'She's trying to breathe fire but nothing's coming out,' said Archie.

'It's toasting time, Sky Dragon,' said Leon.

'You should have joined us when you had the chance,' said Vainclaw.

As one, the Kinghorns took a deep breath and sent four powerful jets of fire at Nebula. Archie shielded Holly from the heat. It was so hot he felt like his back was being cooked but when he looked up he saw that the flames had been stopped.

The Kinghorns stood behind a wall of fire the width of the building and twenty metres high. They looked confused by what had happened. In front of them, Nebula held her open paws inside the wall as though holding it up, apparently immune to the heat of the fire.

'Leon, fly over it,' ordered Vainclaw.

Leon shot into the sky but as he tried to get over the firewall, Nebula waved a paw, sending a burst of fire in the shape of a dragon's head into his lower chin. The smell of burning dragon flesh filled the air and Leon tumbled back down, still on the same side of the wall.

'Eh, bro, you've burnt your nose,' laughed Mali.

'You two, go around it,' demanded Vainclaw.

Mali and Delfina took a side each but, this time, Nebula moved both paws, causing giant claws of flame to shoot out either side, scorching their wings and sending them back to where they had started.

'Eh, ar kid,' said Leon. 'You've burnt your wing.'

'Shut your mouth.'

'You shut yours.'

'Both of you, be quiet,' said Vainclaw, pacing. 'This firewall won't last long. Once it has burnt away, we will take her apart without fire. We will use our teeth and our claws.'

Nebula opened her mouth and breathed a fresh burst of fire into the flaming wall. She made another movement with her paws and the firewall curled round at the edges, encircling and entrapping the Kinghorns in the centre of the building.

'I fear the humans of this city may have noticed my firewall. They will be looking up, therefore I suggest you take the box with the sliding doors to leave,' said Nebula.

'You're letting them escape?' said Archie.

'No, I'm asking them to leave. I have no interest in imprisoning these dragons' said Nebula.

'What do you say, bro? Shall we get out of here?' said Mali.

'Yeah, I reckon it's time for a sharp exit, ar kid,' said Leon.

'She is too powerful,' added Delfina.

The three dragons backed away and Leon pressed the lift button.

'You cowards,' said Vainclaw, standing upright and staring angrily at Nebula through the flames. He spread his wings, revealing his right wing, torn and frayed at the edge. He opened his mouth.

'Your Dragonsong is no use here,' said Nebula. 'I can direct the wind to keep the sound away.'

Vainclaw growled, defeated. He dropped to all fours and joined the others in the lift. Mali slipped through the hole in the bottom of the lift to make enough room for him.

'That's right, run away,' said Karnataka. 'Officer Grunling will arrest you as soon as you set foot in the lithosphere tunnel.'

'Balti Grunling?' said Vainclaw. 'Who do you think released Delfina after she was caught spying for me? It's amazing what some Drakes will do for a pot of pepper.'

'I'll kill him,' said Karnataka.

'Nebula Colarado,' said Vainclaw, rearing up once more, 'because of you, when the time comes we will show no mercy to the Sky Dragons. You will all bow down before us.'

The lift doors closed.

The Kinghorns had gone. Nebula lowered her paws and the firewall burnt away to nothing. She turned to look at the others.

'Miss Nebula, I have never seen a firewall before,' said Alba.

'That was really cool,' said Archie, clapping his hands

together.

'Thank you for the sustenance, human,' said Nebula. 'I haven't tasted sugar since the Middle Ages. It's better than I remember.'

'The name's Archie Snellgrove.' He grinned, handing her another jelly bean from his pocket.

'Thank you,' she replied, taking it.

'Did we win?' said a small pained voice.

Holly was lying against Dirk, her leg mangled, her jeans drenched in fresh blood, a look of agony in her eyes.

'Archie Snellgrove, gather up the ash,' commanded Nebula, 'and stay away from the edge. Humans may still be looking.'

'I hope they do not see Mr Captain Karnataka, then,' said Alba.

Archie and Nebula looked up to see the Shade-Hugger flying fast up into the sky, his dark brown back quickly vanishing into the night.

'Never mind him, bring the ash here, cover the leg,' said Nebula, tearing Holly's jeans, exposing her leg. It was bloody and bruised.

Archie scooped up a handful of fine ash, carried it to Holly, opened his fingers and allowed it to pour on to her leg. She gritted her teeth with pain. The ash instantly turned red as the blood soaked through.

'Sorry, Holly,' he said.

'Quickly, cover the leg,' said Nebula.

Archie brought more until the whole leg was covered with blood-red ash.

'Stand back,' said Nebula and he moved back. The Sky Dragon opened her mouth and breathed blue flames, which licked over the ash.

Holly cried out in pain.

'You're hurting her,' said Archie, trying to pull Nebula away.

'No, she is being made all the better. Look,' said Alba, pointing to Holly's leg. The ash was glowing gold under the blue flame and it looked as though the blood was draining back into the leg.

Nebula closed her mouth and the flames vanished. 'The bone is fixed,' she said.

With Archie's help, Holly tried to stand. Tentatively she put some weight on to her leg. She looked up in amazement. 'It's better,' she said. 'How did you do that?'

'Dragon or human, skin or bone, we all need the same things to survive; water, earth, air and fire. It takes fire to mend a broken bone,' said Nebula.

Archie realised he still had his arm around Holly's

shoulder even though her leg was better now. He let go, embarrassed, and said, 'Sorry, you don't need me.'

'I think I do,' said Holly, smiling. 'You saved my life twice. Thanks.'

'The dragons did all the hard work.' Archie grinned. Then, eyes widening, he added, 'Dragons, Holly. There are real dragons. I can't believe it. I knew you were worth following. I knew it.'

'Now, let's see about the one who summoned me,' said Nebula, bending down to inspect Dirk, who still hadn't moved since swallowing the liquid fire.

'It wasn't his fault,' said Holly.

'I know,' said Nebula.

'Will he be all right?' asked Holly.

'He needs water. Hold his mouth open,' said Nebula. She raised her head to the sky and took a long intake of breath.

Alba lifted Dirk's head and prised open his jaws. Holly and Archie watched as a strand of vaporised water fell from a cloud above. Nebula caught it, allowing it to run through her paws and trickle into Dirk's open mouth as pure, cool fresh water.

Dirk coughed.

He spluttered.

His eyes opened and he sat up.

'Dirk, you're all right,' said Holly, throwing her arms around him.

'Hey, kiddo,' he replied, smiling.

'I'm sorry, Mr Dirk,' said Alba.

'That's OK, Alba.' He looked at Nebula and said, 'I'm sorry too; they forced me to summon you.'

'These are complicated times I have materialised into,' she said, nodding. 'My name is Nebula Colorado.'

'Pleased to meet you, Nebula, I'm Dirk Dilly. It's not safe for you here. Are you able to sublimate again?' he asked.

'Not until I have bathed in the Outer Core and regained enough strength.'

Dirk stood up, carefully checking that everything was in working order.

'Alba,' he said, 'take Nebula somewhere remote where she can safely head underground without being seen.'

'OK, Mr Dirk. I am sorry I deceived you. I just wanted to save Delfina, but now I know that it is too late for her,' she said sadly.

'It's just Dirk,' he replied, 'and, Alba . . .'

'Yes, Mr Dirk?'

'Stick to the ocean from now on. I don't think you're suited to city life.'

'Yes, Mr Dirk.'

'Many thanks for the coloured sugar, Archie Snellgrove,' said Nebula.

'Yes, I very liked your jelly beans too,' added Alba.

Archie dug around in his pocket and pulled out his last two jelly beans, one red, one green. He wiped off the fluff.

'Here,' he said, holding them up for Alba and Nebula, 'for the journey.'

'You can have the red if you like,' said Alba.

'I prefer the green,' replied Nebula, taking the sweet. 'Thank you, Archie Snellgrove. Until the next time.'

'What next time?' said Archie.

'The next time we meet,' said Nebula, looking at him with her milk-white eyes.

'I hope we will be meeting again too,' said Alba. 'I will let you ride on my back again if you bring more jelly beans.'

Archie grinned. 'I hope so too,' he said. 'Goodbye, Alba.'

Nebula and Alba flapped their wings and took to the air, hovering above the roof.

'Thanks for fixing my leg,' said Holly.

'You are most welcome,' replied Nebula. 'Part of me is now part of you and lives in your bone. Remember me with the steps you take.'

'I will,' said Holly.

'Maybe next time we'll have more time to talk,' said Dirk.

'I fear we won't,' replied Nebula. 'Goodbye.'

Holly and Archie waved as the two dragons flew straight up, disappearing into the night sky.

'That's so cool,' said Archie.

'Yes it is.' Dirk nodded. 'So are you two ready?'

They both climbed on his back, Holly with her arms around Dirk's neck, Archie holding on to her. Dirk spread his wings. He checked that no one was looking and glided down towards London, on his way home.

'So this is normal for you, is it?' said Archie, 'chasing dragons and saving the world?'

'It's the summer holiday,' replied Holly. 'What else is there to do?'

Chapter Thirty

As no one knows for sure whether Sky Dragons really can create firewalls, no one knows for sure how they work. One theory popular amongst dragon historians, however, is that Sky Dragons are so attuned to the air particles that surround them that they are able to manipulate them using their breath and paws. To create a firewall, the theory goes, they isolate the oxygen that is present in the air and purify it. As pure oxygen is flammable, it only takes a flame to ignite it and for that section of the air to become a burning wall of fire. This would also explain other powers sometimes attributed to Sky Dragons, such as the ability to draw

water particles from clouds, and to deflect harmful
sounds away, such as Dragonsong.

Dirk looked up from the book. He was sitting on the roof across the road from the art gallery. The double-chinned security guard was fast asleep in front of the screens, snoring, with his hand inside the doughnut box.

Dirk Dilly's was a lonely occupation. Unlike other jobs, he didn't have colleagues to discuss last night's telly or the football results or the price of beans, so sometimes he would spend so much time secretly watching someone, like the double-chinned security guard, that he came to think of him a bit like a colleague. He was a reassuringly familiar face.

Had the double-chinned security guard known that a four-metre-long (from nose to tail), red-backed, green-bellied, urban-based Mountain Dragon thought of his face as reassuringly familiar, he would probably have fallen off his chair and dropped his doughnut.

When Dirk had said goodbye to Holly and lowered her into her bedroom window late Tuesday night he had expected to see her the following day or, at least, the next week, but as he lingered on her roof he heard shouting.

'Where have you been?' he heard her dad's big-haired wife yelling. 'Your father has been worried sick. What time do you call this? Why are your jeans torn? What a state! You look like you've been to war.'

Holly's response was too quiet for Dirk to hear but he could detect her tone: stubborn, determined and quietly angry.

The next day she had called. 'They're having steel bars put on the window,' she said.

'Steel's no problem,' said Dirk, snapping his jaws together.

'They'll get really suspicious if you break the bars. No, I'm stuck here for the whole holiday,' said Holly, trying not to sound too glum. 'It was worth it though. We stopped Vainclaw, and Buchanan won't be able to use the earthquake weapon without the instructions.'

'I'm just relieved he doesn't know about my lot,' said Dirk. 'Fighting Kinghorns is one thing but if a human as rich and powerful as Buchanan knew the truth about dragons life would get very complicated.'

Dirk looked out of his window. The clouds that had marred the beginning of the holidays had gone now and the summer had properly kicked in. He felt bad for Holly stuck inside while everyone else in London was down the park, playing ball games, having picnics, or simply lolling, enjoying the glorious sunshine.

'At least they're letting Archie visit me,' she said. 'I think they don't want to discourage me from making friends. Look, I'd better go, I'm not supposed to be making phone calls without permission.'

'OK, call me soon,' he said, putting the receiver down, feeling something he hadn't felt before. It was an emotion he recognised from his work as a detective. He felt jealous. He begrudged Archie getting to spend time with Holly when he couldn't see her.

Something caught his eye inside the security room. He looked up. The row of security cameras had gone fuzzy.

He checked the street below and flew to the large window, which he pushed open, and climbed into the gallery, holding one paw over his nose to stop the trail of smoke from triggering the alarm.

Looking around the room, he spotted a camera-neutraliser in the corner of the gallery. On the floor was the painting of the sad-looking lady. It was moving exactly as before but this time it was heading back towards the spot where it had originally been stolen from. The picture was being returned.

Dirk stooped down and lifted up the moving painting. Underneath were six white mice. They had metallic collars around their necks and tiny mechanical devices on their backs. Four of them were equipped with electronic clips that allowed them to carry the stolen picture. One had a glass cutter. Dirk picked up another and inspected the grappling hook it was carrying. *So that's how they got the picture down from the wall*, he thought. The mouse between his paws didn't struggle and Dirk would have thought it not real if it wasn't for the tiny heartbeat he could feel.

He looked more closely at the device on its back and saw in very small lettering, a G and an S printed in dark blue formed into a circle.

Dirk was so stunned to see the Global Sands logo that he forgot to keep his paw over his nose. He didn't notice as a thin line of grey smoke escaped from his right nostril, drifting up through the room, into the vent in a small white box on the ceiling, setting off the fire alarm.

'Sweet rats from Sweden. Not again . . .' he swore, dropping the mouse, running across the room and leaping out of the window before the security guard came charging into the gallery.

The next morning Dirk phoned the gallery and asked for Mr Strettingdon-Smythe.

'Ah, Mr Dilly,' said the plummy-voiced curator. 'I was just going to call you. You'll never guess what has happened.'

'One of the stolen paintings has been returned?' he ventured.

'Oh, you did guess,' said Mr Strettingdon-Smythe. 'Yes, the sad-looking lady was returned last night. It's very peculiar. Can you understand it?'

'I'm beginning to get the picture,' said Dirk, inwardly groaning at his own pun. 'When you called me you said your boss didn't want you to contact anyone.'

'That's right. He said it would be bad for business.'

'And may I ask the name of your boss?' Dirk asked, pouring himself a glass of neat orange squash.

'The gallery is owned by Global Sands. Brant Buchanan himself forbade me from calling anyone.'

Dirk knocked the orange squash back in one. 'My advice to you would be to wait. In time all the paintings will be returned.'

'But what's going on?' Mr Strettingdon-Smythe barked.

'It's safer for you if you don't know,' said Dirk firmly.

It was clear to him now that Buchanan was using the art gallery as a training ground for his mouse thieves. That's why he wouldn't allow the curator to call the police. He was stealing from himself. The metallic collars the mice wore must have enabled him to control them remotely, turning them into unwitting mini criminals. Mice could get in anywhere and with enough of them they could steal anything from a painting to a secret government weapon.

'Have a good day, Mr Strettingdon-Smythe.' Dirk put the phone down and switched on the morning news.

'. . . after days of speculation regarding the strange sightings on top of Centre Point in London last Tuesday, the mystery has finally been solved,' the female newsreader was saying. 'A spokesperson for Gronkong Shinard PLC, the company which owns the top floor and roof of the building, explained that they had been testing new weather-predicting equipment at the time.'

Dirk sat back and bit open a tin of beans.

'And now back to our main story,' continued the newsreader in a sing-song voice. 'Volcanologists are trying to explain why three volcanoes, thought to be dormant, have erupted simultaneously . . .'

Images of flowing lava and ash clouds came on screen.

'. . . In a strange coincidence, all three volcanoes were situated on islands owned by Brant Buchanan, the seventh richest man in the world. Although no one was hurt in the eruptions, the islands have endured severe damage. Mr Buchanan was unavailable for comment but a Global Sands spokesman said, "Thankfully, Mr Buchanan has a fully comprehensive insurance policy that covers the damage."'

In another part of London, in the back of his Bentley, Brant Buchanan was also watching the news report, laughing, clapping his hands together.

'How are the share prices, Weaver?' he asked.

Weaver's face appeared on the plasma screen. 'It looks like it's worked, sir,' he said. 'The insurance pay-out for the three islands is so big that the share prices for the insurance company are plummeting, meaning you can purchase the company at a bargain price.'

Sensing the disapproval in his employee's voice, Buchanan said, 'You think it's extravagant to erupt three volcanoes in order to buy an insurance company on the cheap, don't you, Weaver?'

'I think some would call it extravagant,' replied the driver, choosing his words carefully.

'What would you call it?'

'I'd call it a rich man's hobby,' he said.

'It's lucky you made a copy of the instructions,' said Buchanan. 'Talking of which, let's have a look at that security tape.'

The image of Weaver's face slid to the side of the screen and grainy CCTV footage appeared, showing three angles of the upstairs office in the lab. Across the bottom of the screen ran the time.

19:44:58 . . .

19:44:59 . . .

At 19:45:00 something about the size of a golf ball dropped into the room.

'It was rather bold of these thieves to use our own camera-neutraliser to break into the office,' said Buchanan.

'Luckily, as it was our own equipment I was able to isolate the scrambling frequency and recover the picture,' said Weaver. 'The thief should be entering any second.'

Brant Buchanan wasn't used to being surprised. He wasn't surprised when Malcolm Bigsby had told him the location of the VE 6.2 in exchange for a good job with a generous salary. He wasn't surprised that Weaver's remote-controlled mice had successfully stolen the weapon. He wasn't surprised when the weapon actually worked, giving him the single biggest insurance payout in history.

But his jaw literally dropped as he watched, on the CCTV footage, from three different angles, a real, live dragon fall into the picture. The dragon glanced around, surveying the room. Weaver paused the footage on his large face, as it looked directly into one of the cameras. In spite of his childhood fantasies, Brant Buchanan had never dreamt that dragons actually existed, let alone that one had broken into his office. But there it was in front of him. Evidence.

The billionaire leant forward to get a closer look. 'What have we here?' he uttered.

'I'd say you have a new hobby,' replied Weaver drily.